Mind
Over
Murder

Evelyn David

Trace Evidence Press
ISBN-13: 978-0692241080
ISBN-10: 0692241086

DEDICATION

From MEB – With love and deepest gratitude
to my husband John, who has always encouraged and
supported my dreams. You make the hard times easier and
the good times even better.

From Rhonda – To my family for believing I could do it
and for putting up with me while I tried.

.

ACKNOWLEDGMENTS

Many thanks to the Evelyn David fans who have encouraged and supported our writing. We appreciate that you have had faith in us, even when we have had doubts.

CHAPTER 1

"I don't think you were this paranoid before we got married. I would have noticed and believe me it would have been a deciding factor in my decision to hook up with you."

"I'm not paranoid. I'm just cautious and you know as well as I that all is not what it seems. We don't need GPS. A paper map works just fine. Besides, I don't want to be tracked by satellites. You've seen those drones on the news? How do you think they find their targets?"

"Who would bother to track us? Besides, we're going in circles. Why don't you pull over and ask for directions. That should be safe enough."

"Just check the map again, please...dear. And we are not going in circles!"

"I don't need to check the map again...sweetheart. And you are driving in circles. We've passed that French restaurant three times." I loved him but my husband wasn't the most observant man in the world.

"Are you sure? Might be a chain. If you could learn to read a map...."

Neither was he the most patient. "I told you to take the Milton exit, Jake. You completely ignored me."

"You told me too late. I would have had to take out a semi and a 10-year old Ford to get in the right lane in time to make that exit."

"You should have let me drive. I'm a better driver." I really wasn't but it irritated him no end when I made that claim.

"Read my mind."

"Is that an invitation?" I smiled at him. "You know how much you hate it when–"

"Damn it, Valentine, we're going to be late. Where's the next exit that will get us to the church?"

Okay. It was time to let him off the hook. He wasn't going to be disappointed since neither of us really liked going to weddings. They remind us too much of our own.

"It doesn't matter. The groom is on a plane to Mexico City. No one is going to notice we're not there."

"Peter is dumping Allison at the altar? Are you sure?"

"Yeah. I had a dream. Peter was sitting on a plane, reading today's paper, and the seat next to him was empty." I shook my head. "Aunt Delia is going to have a fit. She and Uncle Calvin spent a mint on Allison's dress. I told her not to, but like you, she never listens to me."

He glanced over at me, eyes narrowed. "So you knew about this for some time?"

"Maybe." I wasn't admitting anything. He gets annoyed with me telling him how things are going to turn out so I generally try to keep my premonitions to myself unless I thought the information was absolutely vital. Sometimes what I thought was vital and his definition of vital varied. This might have been one of those times.

"No maybe about it. You didn't think of mentioning it to me? Maybe before I put on this monkey suit?"

"No. Besides, I thought as long as we were both dressed up we could go somewhere nice for dinner." I gave him my best beseeching look. "I made reservations at Josephine's."

"That French restaurant we keep driving by?"

"See how well that worked out?"

***

The doorbell chimed drawing my attention away from the computer screen and the bid I was about to place for Jake on a 1939 New York World's Fair medallion pin. Jake and his nemesis Newton548 were in a bidding war for the item. Five minutes were left in the on–line auction and Jake was losing.

I looked up at the couple entering the shop. The woman was in her early forties, short blonde hair, no-nonsense manner. The guy was slightly younger or maybe his attitude was younger. His hair was brushing his shoulders and his beard was in the awkward stage. They picked their way through the stacked wooden crates that Jake hadn't gotten around to unpacking; the spoils of our recent trip to the antique mecca of New Hope, Pennsylvania. The man turned sideways in order to slide between the boxes. His suit jacket flipped open as it snagged on a crate and I caught a glimpse of his shoulder holster. Cops or rather detectives. Wonderful. Newton548 was going to chalk up another win. Jake would just have to deal with it.

"Can I help you?"

"Are you Valerie Zalmanzig?" the man asked.

I shook my head. "Nope." Everyone always tried to twist my first name into something they recognized, something more common. And while Zalmanzig was the name I was born with, when I married Jake almost five years ago, I acquired a white elephant of a house, a disapproving mother-in-law, and since there is always a bright side to most things–a surname with no z's.

"If you're not Zalmanzig, who are you?" The female detective's eyes flashed.

It didn't take any special abilities to see that she didn't believe me. Probably had a photograph of me in a file on her desk. I could see her ticking off the details: thirty-two year old Caucasian female; five-foot-five inches tall; long red hair; and hostile, brown eyes (a by-product of my dealings with law enforcement). After my last dance with the local police department, I'd told the Chief in no uncertain terms that I wouldn't be available for consultations in the future. Obviously, the Chief had conveniently forgotten.

I sighed. In the shower this morning Jake had warned me that he had a bad feeling about today. I thought he was just annoyed that he had to use my lavender scented bath gel.

The male cop shifted and almost knocked a 1950s floor lamp into an opened crate of Japanese porcelain. He caught the lamp but I didn't see him do it. Instead I saw a shattered teacup lying in a pool of red on a polished wooden floor.

Not my cup. Not my floor.

"Your name, please."

The female cop's words drew me back. Someone was dead.

I blinked once, then cleared my throat. "Who wants to know?"

They both pulled out gold shields and waved them in front of me. I snagged the woman's before she stuck it back in her blazer pocket. Glancing from the shield to the ID card, I read her name aloud, "Detective Diane Ellison."

Detective Ellison nodded. "And my partner is–"

"Mike Hardesty," I mumbled, his name popping into my mind before she could say the words.

Whoops.

I glanced up.

They smiled.

Damn. Me and my big mouth.

I handed the badge back. I shouldn't have touched it.

***

"It's been five years. I'm retired," I repeated, ripping open a package of Oreo cookies and dumping them onto a platter. I handed the platter to Detective Hardesty and turned to check on the coffee that was dripping into the glass carafe. As I watched, the brown drips turned to red.

Blood.

I blinked. Blood was dripping off a woman's hand onto a broken teacup.

"Chief Peterson mentioned that you might be reluctant to help us," Hardesty mumbled, between bites of cookie. "She said to tell you she's willing to let bygones be bygones. She says everyone is entitled to one mistake."

The detective's voice was getting farther and farther away. I could see the blood trailing down the woman's bare arm to her hand.

"It's a mistake. You've made a mistake." The words echoed in my mind. The voice wasn't the detective's. It was an older man's and he wasn't talking to me. He was talking to someone holding a knife.

Detective Ellison touched my sleeve. "Miss Zalmanzig?"

The knife flashed and blood spurted onto a bedroom wall–an obscene design on the white paint.

The killer opened a window and stared angrily out into the snowy night.

"Miss Zalmanzig?"

The blue-striped wallpaper was gone. It was the same wall as five years ago but the wallpaper was gone, replaced by white paint. And fresh blood.

I focused on the Detective. "It's Mrs. Cohen. The Chief arrested the wrong man five years ago. I told her. She didn't believe me."

I couldn't wait for the carafe to fill. Time was running out. I grabbed it and coffee splattered onto the warming plate, the hot liquid flowing onto the white tiled countertop. I watched the liquid change again from brown to red. More people had died because I'd failed before.

Ellison took the carafe from me and jammed it back in the machine. Hardesty grabbed a cloth from the counter and mopped at the mess.

"She knows," Hardesty said, his voice soft as he soaked up the coffee into one of Jake's mother's best dish towels. "The Chief knows the mistake wasn't yours. Fletcher is still on death row but we've got another couple murdered."

Mostly just to keep myself grounded, and already knowing the answer, I asked a question. "In the old Chang house?"

"Yeah, but the couple living there now...." Ellison sighed. "Sorry, the couple that was killed last night was named Berman."

Hardesty tossed the wet towel into the sink.

I was going to catch hell over the coffee stains. Jake's mother was very particular about her things–and her son. She wasn't going to like this. Not one little bit. "Both stabbed? Both killed in the master bedroom?"

The female detective nodded. "It's just like last time."

I picked up the towel from the sink and began rinsing it out. I needed to act before the stain set. I needed to find the killer before someone else died. This time I couldn't stop until I found the truth.

CHAPTER 2

"Do you want a salad?" I didn't wait for his answer, just pulled out a head of lettuce from the crisper drawer along with a sack of carrots.

Jake finished turning the rib-eye steaks that were cooking under the oven broiler before responding—and when he did speak it wasn't about food. "I thought we agreed when we got married that you wouldn't get involved in any more murder investigations."

I used a large knife to chop the ends off three carrots that were past their prime. The knife striking the vegetables made a satisfying thump on the wooden cutting board. "I didn't go looking for this; the police came to me, remember?"

"It's not too late to say *no* to them. They can't force you to get involved."

"I'm already involved. I've been involved since that first couple was murdered in their bed five years ago. I couldn't pinpoint the killer then, but I knew it wasn't the guy the cops arrested. Alex Fletcher was a lot of things, including a murderer, but he didn't kill the Changs. No one would believe me then. They might now."

Jake appeared at my side and put his hand over mine, stilling the knife. "Are you sure it's not a copycat killer? That cable thriller about the Chang murders was re-aired about a week ago."

"I'm sure." I paused, then added, "The police are sure. The Chief wouldn't have reached out and admitted her mistake if she wasn't sure."

"From what you've told me, she hasn't exactly admitted she made a mistake." Jake raised his eyebrows. "Two days ago you were sure that Peter and Allison weren't getting married. Turns out Peter was on a plane all right, but so was Allison. The little detail about an elopement didn't show up in your dream. So maybe you're wrong about this too. You don't always know, Valentine. This could be a different murderer–just a coincidence that a second couple was killed in the same house."

I frowned. I didn't like his habit of rubbing my face in my mistakes. It wasn't one of his most attractive traits. But before I could come up with an appropriately pithy reply he continued.

"And the police? The Chief is sure? She was also sure that Fletcher was guilty. I followed the case. Hell, the whole town did. The police found his fingerprints in the bedroom. When they finally tracked him down in Dallas, he still had some of the things he stole from the Changs in his car. The guy was stone cold guilty."

"Guilty of lots of things–but not of killing the Changs. Fletcher admitted to robbing the couple the day before the murders. He'd repaired the chimney on their house and when they weren't looking had taken more than just a check in payment. But he's always denied killing them." I stared into his eyes, willing him to understand. "It's past time that I finished this. Will you help me?"

"No." He sighed and released my hand. "But I won't stand in your way. I know you're going to do what you want to do anyway, regardless of what I want."

"Jake?" I wasn't sure if he was angry or just afraid for me; afraid of the toll I would pay for traveling in a murderer's wake. We'd met during the Fletcher trial. He'd seen what the fallout had been for me. He'd been my safe haven when the police chief had thrown me to the media wolves.

I'd lost a lot getting involved in the Chang Murders. My career, my reputation, and most of my friends. I had a Master's Degree in psychology. I'd been the star of the biggest jury consulting firm in New York. Attorneys were anxious to hire me because of my "amazing insight" into jury makeup, trial strategy, even the innocence or guilt of their clients. Local police departments quietly hired me as a consultant for difficult cases. Of course, I'd never mentioned to anyone my other "talents," my visions of past and future. But when a national rag sheet plastered my face on the cover and called me a fake who traded on the tragedies of others, the firm quickly cut all ties with me. I couldn't get hired to tell fortunes in a carnival once the tabloids, local, national, as well as television shows were done with me. I don't know what I would have done without Jake. Meeting him and falling in love saved me.

"Honey, I need to do this."

"Right!" Jake walked back over to the oven. "Did I mention that I talked to my mother today? She sends her regards."

He was bringing up his mother? Now? I glanced over at his stiff back. He wasn't afraid for me. He was angry. He was definitely angry. I chopped the carrots up in record time. Fine. I could deal with that. Two could play the game. "Did I mention that Newton548 outbid you on that medallion you wanted?"

***

I bunched up my pillow and stuck it back under my head. Staring upward, I tried to isolate the exact moment when the day had first gone wrong. Ever since I was a kid, I'd been convinced that bad days were the result of one mistake, one misstep that derailed the whole day, and that if I could only identify it, future bad days could be avoided. This theory, although not without major flaws, had served me well enough that I continued to use it. Assuming that stubbing my big toe on the bathroom door at 3 AM didn't count, it had to have been the 7 AM conversation with my Aunt Sarah. As usual she and Momma were squabbling over something that had happened when they were both teenagers. It was a strange week when one or the other of them didn't call me from Oklahoma just to complain about the other. But this time instead of agreeing to talk to Momma and smooth the waters, I'd told Aunt Sarah in no uncertain terms that I wasn't going to be the go-between for them any more–that she and Momma could call Aunt Delia instead. At least Aunt Delia had been a witness to their childhood! Of course the problem was Aunt Delia would remember the incident differently than either of them and wouldn't hesitate a second to tell them that they were both wrong. That kind of information wasn't anything Momma or Aunt Sarah wanted to hear. Of course Aunt Sarah wasn't pleased with my response either or at least that's what I took the "you always were an ungrateful little twit" comment to mean. So my dealings with my aunt might have set the tone for the day–that or Jake's ill humor about the lavender shower gel.

I could hear him brushing his teeth. Jake always brushed them extra-long when he was angry with me. He was taking his sweet time coming to bed. I didn't think he was mad enough to sleep in the guest room but it had always been hard for me to judge his feelings correctly. His emotions tended to change like quicksilver and I was always a step behind in deciphering them. I'm really not as good at reading his mind as he thinks I am.

Over dinner he'd made clear his very rational reasons for why another murder investigation was a really bad idea. He brought up the nightmares and the migraines and the half dozen psychosomatic illnesses that I'd endured while grappling with the psychic messages. He didn't want to watch me go through it again. Hell, I didn't want to go through it again. And I didn't want to think about how it might affect our marriage. We had enough problems without adding a murder investigation to the mix.

The wind outside picked up and the old house shuddered. The sprawling four-storied house had been in the Cohen family for over a hundred years, expanding as each generation had built on an extra room or two. Jake had mentioned more than once that he'd probably add on something, just to keep with tradition. He'd hinted several times about a second nursery in the wing that housed the antique shop. Talking about a second nursery when we didn't have any occupants for the first nursery seemed too much like tempting fate to me. I usually changed the subject when he brought it up.

The bathroom light went out leaving only the full moon to illuminate the bedroom. My eyes were slow to adjust. I couldn't see the cracks in the ceiling but I knew they were there, just above my head. Among the other problems, the house's foundation was crumbling. It seemed to me that the cracks were getting wider and deeper every day. Jake and I needed to fix them before it was too late.

My husband slipped into bed beside me and stuck his Popsicle feet against the back of my bare calves.

I grinned and turned towards him. He might be angry, but he wasn't too angry.

Despite everything I loved Jake Cohen and I know he loved me. What were a few cracks compared to that?

***

The yellow crime scene tape danced in the wind and the snow began to fall. Another storm was about to blow in from the west. Seamont had already had its fair share of snow for the season. The historic town had grown up during the early 1900s as a summer vacation spot for the city dwellers. The ocean breezes made for a temperate summer but harsh winters. Most of the houses were built with large verandas and windows to catch the sea views. They were impossible to heat in the winter. When the village was first built, the population of Seamont dropped by half by the end of October, not to increase until again until early May. Now Seamont was a trendy commuter town to the Big Apple, just 40 minutes from Grand Central via Metro-North.

Jake's family had been one of the few to live in Seamont year-round. Even after we'd invested a fortune in thermal windows and insulation, parts of the house were virtually unlivable in the winter. Of course some drafts and cold spots weren't due to the weather.

"Come inside with me please." I knew I was pushing my luck. Jake had offered to drive me to the Chang house– it would always be the Chang house in my mind–but he hadn't changed his stance about not getting involved in the investigation.

He picked up a newspaper from the car seat and inclined his head towards the house where the two detectives were waiting for me. "You'll have plenty of company. I'll sit out here and check out the classifieds. See if there are any estate sales coming up. I assume we're still going to Boston next weekend?"

"Absolutely. I'm not going to shirk my half of the work at the shop."

"That's not what I'm worried about." He crooked a finger at me and I leaned in for a quick goodbye kiss.

"I know. I'm sorry." I opened the car door and got out, taking care not to slip on the icy sidewalk. I was sorry. Sorry that our lives weren't as simple as Jake would prefer. Sorry his mother didn't like me. And sorrier than I could say that I hadn't found the Changs' killer before he had killed again.

***

Detective Ellison was the skeptic. She stood out of the way but watched every move I made. I think she was afraid I was going to steal the Bermans' silver. Maybe not steal exactly, but she didn't trust me. Detective Hardesty was the true believer. He hovered near my elbow, his notebook out, waiting for me to start spouting clues. I think I disappointed both of them. Most of the Bermans' furnishings weren't old enough to be interesting or new enough to be worth much. There were some pieces that I felt belonged to someone else? The Changs? I wasn't able to get a clear reading. And to Detective Hardesty's dismay, I didn't hear any disembodied voices shouting the killer's name and social security number the minute he ushered me in the door.

I had visited the Chang house in December, five years before, at the behest of Chief Liza Peterson. Newly appointed, Peterson was intent on finding the person who had broken into Lee and Vera Chang's home one snowy night and stabbed them each more than a dozen times. She'd heard of me from a police chief in New Jersey whom I'd helped in a kidnapping case. Liza Peterson might have had the best of intentions, but when the news got out that she had a psychic working the case, she hadn't been able to stand up to the ridicule. One morning after a particularly scathing news story, she'd left a message on my answering machine that my services were no longer needed. Back then I wasn't strong enough to get through to her and the wrong man went to prison. I hadn't been back to the house since. But the killer had.

The staircase was the same as before. Polished oak banister. Dark green carpet on the stairs. Rage permeating the air, thicker near the top.

I paused on the sixth step. The killer had paused there too. Both times. Why? I couldn't see past the second floor landing. The step didn't squeak any alarm.

"Are you getting something?" Detective Hardesty bumped into me, then clumsily moved back down a step.

Besides a headache? I looked behind me and caught Detective Ellison's eye. She understood my problem.

"Mike, give her some space. You're blocking the vibes from reaching her."

"Wow." Detective Hardesty looked around as though the vibes in question might be visible; something he might need to brush off his shoulders.

I smiled in relief as he backed two more steps farther down the stairs. "Thanks." I noticed that now the six-foot detective's head was level with mine.

A thought really did strike me—well metaphorically at least. I went up two steps and stopped. I could see the master bedroom door.

"The killer is tall. At least six foot, likely taller. And probably male."

"Wow." Detective Hardesty stared at me and then backed away another step. I guess he was hoping more distance would yield more data.

I couldn't see a downside to leaving him with that belief.

***

"Mrs. Cohen? Are you all right?"

My knees ached. I opened my eyes and realized I was kneeling on the wooden floor of the bedroom. I was in the same spot where the killer had stood looking down at his slain victims.

They were just another obstacle between him and what he wanted. He hated them. He resented the time he'd had to waste on them. Both emotions, anger and frustration, filled the room, stronger even than the cold terror that clung to the four-poster bed.

I wished again that Jake had come in with me. I was going to need his strength. I was going to need his help.

CHAPTER 3

"Do you mind if my mother joins us for lunch?" Jake asked at the very moment I realized the car had stopped moving.

I opened my eyes and saw our garage door through the front windshield. I was surprised that I'd managed to fall asleep during the short trip; the Chang house was only a couple of miles away from ours.

"Fine, but you know she won't eat a bite of anything I fix."

"Funny." He sighed. "I'd really like the two of you to get along better."

"She doesn't like me."

"I think you can work around that if you try." He grinned. "I don't think she really dislikes you, she just doesn't think you're good enough for her highly intelligent, incredibly handsome, extra special, only son."

I glared at him.

He laughed. "Promise to be nice and I'll go with you this afternoon to the police station.

I gave him a weak smile, then opened the car door and got out. I was going to hold him to that bargain. I had a headache straight from hell and a visit from Ruth Cohen wasn't going to help matters.

Plus I had plumbers coming in a half hour.

***

"I'm moving into my own place soon."

Richard Baez was telling me a story he'd told many times before, with the same ending. He was still living with his parents. We were standing in the utility room of the house, which was behind the shop. I'd noticed a stain on the floor a week earlier, but had been hoping it would go away. It hadn't. It was spreading.

The twenty-something assistant plumber was gesturing with a socket wrench in one hand and a Phillips screwdriver in the other. "I've got it all planned. Big couch, 50-inch TV, fridge full of beer. You'll have to come over and help me decorate." He gave me a look that made my stomach turn.

It was a good thing his father, Javier Baez, was a crackerjack plumber. Richard was tall, greasy black hair, and always smelled like weed. He'd been working with his father for at least 10 years and still hadn't gotten his license. Javier didn't let him handle any jobs alone. Hell, Richard wasn't even that good at handing his father the tools he needed. At the moment Javier was outside getting something from his truck, a job Richard should have been able to handle, but apparently wasn't.

The dinger on the oven timer had been ringing for at least five minutes, I couldn't put it off any longer, even though I hated leaving Richard unsupervised in the shop. "Look, I've got to check on something in the oven. Call me if anyone comes into the store."

Richard gave me a smug smile. "No problem. I'll cover the shop for you. I'll check out those comic books you've got in that box on the counter. I saw an old Superman on top."

"Don't touch them. They're expensive first-editions."

"Oh, come on. They're just comic books." Richard sounded like a whiny nine-year-old.

The smell of a burning chicken casserole made me hustle up the steps. "I mean it. Don't touch anything."

I was about five minutes too late. The breaded topping of the casserole was scorched. I was trying to figure out if any of it was salvageable when I heard Richard calling me.

It wasn't a customer.

"The oil tank is leaking." The elder Baez slid out from under the cast iron behemoth oil tank that took up half the furnace room. He wiped his oil-stained hands on his jeans. I felt like Javier, and the ever-present Richard, had been practically living with us since Jake and I had been married. Something was always leaking or broken.

I sighed. This old house was a money pit.

"Can it be patched?"

Richard didn't even try to contain his laughter.

I glared at him, which was nothing compared to the look he got from his father. The young man didn't look the slightest bit embarrassed, but he did shut up.

Javier was in his early 60s, heavy-set and gray-haired, I'd never seen him smile. He was very serious about plumbing and just about everything else in life. His brow seemed permanently furrowed. I guess since Richard was his only child, a few wrinkles were inevitable.

"No ma'am. If it were a line or a fitting, then maybe. But it's the tank. You got to replace it."

I looked around the small room behind the shop that housed the ancient furnace, oil tank, and the water heater which Javier had assured me was also on its last legs. It suddenly occurred to me that the shop had been built long after the furnace had been installed.

"How do you get the old tank out of here and a new one in?"

Richard interrupted. "Only way out is through the shop. We'll take the door to this room off the hinges and see if that gives us enough room. If not, we'll cut open the sheetrock to widen the opening."

The young man seemed excited at the prospect of major demolition.

Jake wasn't going to like this. Not only was it going to be expensive, but we were going to have to close for several days. Plus the shop itself was going to have to be rearranged to allow Javier and Richard to go in and out. And worst of all, I was going to have to listen to Richard's innuendos and potty humor for at least a week.

***

I'd gotten lucky and my mother-in-law had postponed her visit. Something about urgent business elsewhere. Thank God. Between the furnace and the police, my patience was wearing thin.

Now I just had to get through the meeting with Chief Peterson without letting past grievances get in the way of catching a killer.

Jake had the windshield wipers going at turbo speed even if the car wasn't. The snow was blowing so hard that visibility was almost zip.

"We could turn around and go home," he suggested. "Build a fire and go through that crate of old books we had shipped back from New Hope from our last buying trip. I picked up some marshmallows at the grocery store yesterday. The tiny ones you like to float in your hot chocolate."

I hid a smile. Jake was the one who liked those marshmallows, but I had to admit that I was tempted. Sorely tempted. And my husband knew it. He really wanted me to bow out of the investigation. I was a little surprised at how strongly he felt about it. Of course with my headache and this weather, it wouldn't take much to convince me to give it up. The vision of him and me curled up on the living room sofa, the fire crackling, the taste of chocolate on his lips as I....

"I'm pretty sure my mother hasn't arrived yet. She said tomorrow."

Splat. That imaginary bubble of bliss was gone. "No, Jake. We should keep going. Chief Peterson is expecting me. I don't want to miss a word of her groveling."

He started to argue but was distracted when a Ford sedan cut in front us going twice what was safe on the slick roads.

"What the...." Jake braked hard and barely managed to keep all four tires on the road. "Did you get the license number? That guy's going to kill someone."

"No. The snow is too thick for me to see the plate. We need to follow him."

He gave me a sharp look. "What?"

"Go faster, Jake. He's pulling away."

"No, Valentine. Absolutely not. I draw the line at chasing speeders. You can't do everything for the police in this town. Let them earn their paychecks."

"I heard a baby crying. It's not his."

***

The blowing snow was both a blessing and a curse; the driver of the Ford didn't realize he was being followed, but we couldn't see much more than the speeding car's taillights.

"I've got a bad feeling about this," Jake complained as he steered into a skid and then skillfully maneuvered our Chevy Tahoe back towards the inside lane.

Translation–he didn't want today to be the day that his brand new pride and joy got its first scratch. I sighed. I'd been through this with him once before. The week of our wedding he'd taken delivery on a new cherry red Pontiac Grand Am; his first new car. The week after our wedding I had backed it out of the garage without first opening the garage door.

Our marriage had gotten off to a rocky start. Jake hadn't yelled but I have a suspicion that he might have checked into the fine print of an annulment. Even after the car was repaired, he never felt the same way about it–or me. Every time he looked at it, I imagined that he was remembering how wonderful the first seven days had been and blaming me for ruining his dream car and picture-perfect marriage. Neither had really been perfect; the car's transmission had been suspect and as his mother had pointed out numerous times, we came from very different backgrounds and religions. But Jake had only seen what he'd wanted to see. I had been relieved when he sold the car to a cousin and bought a used Blazer for our antique shopping trips. Even after five years, that car is something we don't talk about. A week ago he'd traded the Blazer in for a new Chevy Tahoe. Cherry Red.

"We have to stay close enough to see what he does," I warned, as the taillights disappeared.

"Try calling 9-1-1 again."

I looked down at the cell phone I was clutching. "I'm still not getting any signal."

"Is the phone charged? You never remember to charge it."

"Could we argue about this later?" He was right of course about the phone but I was at a loss as to how his observation was going to be helpful in the present circumstances. If he didn't have a thing about carrying one, we'd have a second phone to use.

"Fine, I'll start a list," Jake replied as he flipped the defroster switch to high.

I flinched as the Ford's back end shimmied when it crossed a particularly icy patch.

"Watch out for the–"

"I got it," Jake mumbled, his knuckles whitening as he gripped the steering wheel. "Tell me again–you're sure about the baby? Hell, are you sure the car is stolen? Maybe your circuits are still overloaded from this morning."

"Circuits?" I spared him a glare, then trained my eyes back towards the. "He's turning."

Jake groaned. "This should be interesting–it's a dead end road. Next stop–the Long Island Sound."

***

"Why is he just sitting there?" Jake asked as he slowed the Tahoe to a sliding stop about fifty feet back from the idling Ford.

"I don't know." We had followed the Ford into the deserted waterfront park. The Ford had neared the picnic pavilion, then abruptly stopped.

"Can't you...."

"It doesn't work like that." I rubbed a hand across my dry eyes. I'd been staring at the Ford so hard that I'd forgotten to blink. "Imagine a radio playing in your head. It's always on but won't hold a station for more than a few seconds. Mostly the volume is so low that I can't make out any words, but every once in a while, usually when I'm asleep or upset, the sound turns up and I get whole thoughts or conversations."

"So all you're getting right now is static?"

"Yeah, something like that."

"Okay. So maybe I should get out and go see if the guy needs directions or something. I could pretend that–"

"No. He might panic. He's got a gun."

Jake's head whipped towards me. "You're only now thinking to mention a gun? He could have shot at us anytime during the past ten minutes. If I'd known, I would have—"

"Sorry, but I didn't know about the gun until I said it."

"I've got a full tank of gas."

"Huh?" His abrupt change of subject didn't make sense. Or maybe it just seemed that way since my headache was getting worse.

"I said that I've got plenty of gas so we can sit here until—"

"I can't think, the damn baby keeps screaming its head off. Why is that SUV sitting back there?"

"What?" Jake grabbed my arm. "Valentine?"

"Did I say that out loud?" I blinked and sat up a little straighter in the seat. "I heard him clearly that time."

The snow was getting heavier. I took a quick look around us. I couldn't see the gray ocean water that I knew was only a few hundred feet to our right. The rock picnic pavilion was about ten feet from the Ford. I could just make out the shape of the roof. If the Ford's lights weren't on, I wouldn't have been able to see it at all. Lights! "Shut off our headlights. Turn off the motor."

"Why?"

"So he won't worry about us. If he can't see us, he may think we left."

"And what do you think he's going to do if he thinks we've left?"

"He'll get rid of the baby. He doesn't want to get caught with it."

CHAPTER 4

"He's leaving." Jake swiped at the fogged windshield with one hand, partially clearing the glass. "Did you see him get out of the car?"

"No. Maybe." I unlocked the Tahoe's passenger door. "Let me out here and you follow him."

"Wait a minute. What are you–"

"Follow him, Jake. We need to be sure. I'll check around the pavilion."

I didn't wait to hear his protests, instead I stepped knee-deep into the fresh snow and slammed the Tahoe's door behind me. I think I heard him say something about my manner of closing the door, but I'm sure it was just my imagination. The love of my life couldn't be worrying about his new vehicle at a time like this.

As the Tahoe moved away I was hit by the full force of the winds. Stumbling, I tried to orient myself in the white swirling snow. Straight ahead. I told myself I just had to keep going straight ahead, one foot in front of the other.

Ducking my head, I slowly advanced towards the pavilion, all the while knowing its open sides would offer almost no protection from the weather–not for me and certainly not for an infant.

* * *

My half-frozen hand clutched the rock column, the rough surface a reassuring tactile sensation in the midst of the white-out conditions. I couldn't hear anything but the wind. I couldn't see anything but the snow. I closed my eyes and tried to concentrate, searching for any clue as to the location of the baby.

"Val?"

I turned and found Jake standing beside me, his clothing soaked, a baby car seat dangling from his hand.

"He tossed this in the Sound. Did you find...." The wind caught the rest of his panicked words but I didn't need them.

I took his arm. "We need to get you into some dry clothes and call the police. Let's go find a working phone."

"No, damn it." He shook off my touch. "You do whatever you do. Don't give up because of me."

I stared into his eyes. "Jake, I don't know what to do. I'm not getting anything."

He tossed the seat to the side and knelt down onto the snowdrift-covered floor. "Then we do what normal people do every day. Put out your hands and feel your way through the unknown."

***

The swinging doors opened and Jake walked through. He looked good in green scrubs. Younger. Or maybe it was the big smile on his face that I found so appealing.

I spared a glance at Detective Ellison. She was giving Jake the once over too.

Staking my prior claim, I met him halfway across the waiting room and wrapped my arms around his waist. "Are you, okay? Did you see the baby?"

"We're both great. He's pinking up nicely under that heating lamp. The docs say he's fine."

I grinned. "Detective Ellison says that the baby's name is Christopher Warren. Rudy and Alisha are his frantic parents and they're on their way from Queens courtesy of a New York State Trooper.

"You mean we don't get to keep him?" He laughed and gave me another hug. "I thought there was some rule that if they were over a certain weight or is it length?"

"That's fishing," Detective Ellison joked as she joined us. "You did a good job out there this afternoon Mr. Cohen. If you and Mrs. Cohen hadn't followed that stolen car...." She sighed. "We've got an APB out on the carjacker. But with this weather, it could be days before he's spotted."

***

"Are you ready to go home?" I was worried about Jake. He looked okay but he'd spent a long, wet, ten minutes with me out in the snow storm looking for the baby.

Jake nodded. "More than ready. I'm exhausted."

"We still need to talk about the Berman murders," Detective Ellison said. "Can I come by in a couple of hours?"

I wanted to say no. I even opened my mouth to say no.

The detective quickly added, "I'll bring lasagna from Aurelio's."

Jake perked up immediately. "With their garlic rolls and maybe a cheesecake? I'd be happy to buy, if you'd pick it up."

"I thought you were exhausted." Even if he wasn't, I was. I wasn't in the mood to meet with the detective about the Changs or the Bermans. The weather was getting worse and there was something else....Something else was about to happen. I could feel the pressure behind my eyes building.

He grinned. "Hey, even superheroes have to eat."

Superheroes.

I flashed on the image of a child with a dishcloth cape pinned to his t-shirt. Or maybe it was a her. She or he was small, not more than five or six years old. Curly hair, long for a boy but shorter than a girl would normally wear it. Wanting something that was just out of reach, the child was pondering a jump from the windowsill to the tree limb ten feet below. A door slammed. The child jumped.

"No!" I blinked and the boy or girl was gone. Jake and Detective Ellison were staring at me in surprise. Several other people standing near us looked concerned. Didn't take a psychic to pick up on their thoughts. Crazy person on the loose.

"Valentine?"

"No cheesecake for me; I'm on a diet."

***

"What was that all about?"

He was whispering. It was the first chance we'd had to talk since we'd arrived back at the house. The food was on the table and I was fixing iced tea, the detective declining the wine I'd suggested.

"Last week your mother implied I was getting fat, so I'm trying to cut back on the calories."

"She didn't say you were....Wait a minute; you're trying to distract me. You had a vision!"

"Just a little one." There was no shutting them down now. Quitting the case wasn't an option. Maybe it never was.

"A vision about the baby?"

Okay, I didn't see that coming. "What?"

"Christopher. Was it about him?"

Oh. The baby we rescued. "No. I don't think so. Why would you...." I sighed. "You really bonded with him, didn't you? I know you want a child and maybe I haven't been listening–"

Detective Ellison walked into the kitchen, her cell phone next to her ear. "Right. Two units. I'm on my way and I'll bring her with me. Get the dog guy over there too. If the killer's still in the area, I want him."

I was pretty sure I was the *her* in question. "What's going on?"

"We've had a report of a break-in at the Bermans' house."

"You want me to go with you?"

"Yeah." The detective glanced at the untouched lasagna on the table. "I'm sorry about dinner. But this might be our guy."

CHAPTER 5

"You sure you don't mind?"

Jake gave me a look of disbelief.

"Okay, let me rephrase. I really appreciate you going into the house with me. I know you don't want to–"

"Talk to victims of violent death? No, I don't. But I will, if it means this can be over and we can concentrate on our lives."

"There might not be anyone left in the house." If I really thought that, I wouldn't have asked him to come with me. As far as Detective Ellison knew, Jake was just there to hold my hand. She didn't know about his special talent. No one but his mother and I knew he could see and talk to the dead as easily as the living.

"Valentine, you know that family is one thing, but dealing with strangers and their issues is another. I don't need anything else on my plate. Tomorrow, I'm back to buying and selling antiques."

"Got it," I motioned for him to lean down and I gave him a quick kiss. "Thank you."

"Okay." He brushed the hair out of my eyes. "Let's just get this done. They're ready for you."

I followed his gaze towards Detective Ellison who was motioning for us to join her.

Jake wrapped an arm around my waist. "Remember–"

"I'll keep your secret," I assured him. "Just give me a sign if you need me to distract the cops."

***

Half an hour later, most of the police were gone except for a couple of patrolmen stationed outside the house. Detective Hardesty was down the block, talking to the neighbor who'd called 9-1-1 about someone being in the house. Detective Ellison was sticking close to me. Jake, who was ostensibly waiting outside in the Tahoe, was really upstairs trying to contact ghosts.

As for me, I was trying to ignore the angry emotions the killer had left smeared all over the house; his intense anger and confusion lingering like Pine Sol in the rooms. He'd been back. The killer. No question of that in my mind. For some reason he was compelled to return. But why? His feelings were screaming at me, but they weren't giving me information I could use to identify him.

"How did he get in?" I'd heard all about the neighbor who had decided to give her dog a late night stroll in front of the murder house featured on the evening news. She had seen a light flickering in the upstairs windows and called 9-1-1, excited to claim fifteen minutes of fame.

"Broke a window in back," Detective Ellison answered. "The alarm was turned off because of all the investigators going in and out. We're going to have someone sitting on the house now–at least for the next few weeks.

"Is there a connection between the Changs and the Bermans?" I asked as we wandered into the den. The Bermans were partial to dark blues and grey color schemes. The sectional sofa and assorted chairs were a continuation of the colors used in the more formal living room. A single yellow silk pillow lounged in one chair, a loud, jarring note of cheer.

Detective Ellison shook her head. "Other than the house? Not that we've found. If you remember the Changs were third generation immigrants from China. The family had been in the New York area ever since arriving in the States. The Bermans were originally from Boston, but had spent the last fifteen years in Florida. They retired and moved back north last year. A cousin said they wanted to spend their final years in a place with four seasons."

"I don't guess there is any known connection between the Bermans and Alex Fletcher?"

"No. And believe me the Chief had us searching for one. There's always the chance that the killer is doing Fletcher's bidding; staging a copycat killing to get Fletcher a new trial."

Wishful thinking. Chief Peterson was a stubborn woman. The man on death row for the murder of the Changs was a piece from another jigsaw puzzle all together. Alex Fletcher hadn't been intentionally framed as his defense attorney had claimed; it was more that the chief of police and the district attorney had found a puzzle piece that was the right shade of grey and forced it into the open space in their murder puzzle. Now everything was falling apart because it never really fit.

I wondered what was happening upstairs. I hoped Jake was having a chat with some of the previous owners of the house.

"Mrs. Cohen?" Detective Ellison wanted to show me a photo album she'd just pulled off a shelf in the living room. "Would it help to see a photograph of the Bermans?"

"Why not?" I needed to buy time for Jake. Looking at photographs was as good a way as any.

Lois and George Berman were in their middle sixties but looked ten years younger. The years in Florida had been kind to them. Or maybe it was just good genes. From the notes written under the photos in the album, both Lois and George's parents and grandparents had been alive and active well into their nineties.

"How about children? Grandchildren?"

Detective Ellison nodded and pulled out a second album from the bookcase near the fireplace. "Three daughters. One in northern California and two in Boston. The two in Boston are married. The eldest, Claudia, has teenaged children. The one in California, Beth, is single. A college professor."

I traced my fingers over the glossy images. Claudia, Patricia, no Trish…she liked to be called Trish. I could hear Lois Berman's voice. She had touched these images, telling someone else about her daughters. Someone she didn't know. A man.

Flipping the pages, I paused over the image of two teenagers next to a motorcycle. Lois's words filtered through again. "My granddaughter Gwen and her boyfriend, Toby. My daughter Claudia doesn't like him. Thinks his view of the world is too dark."

I could hear the man laughing. His laugh was too loud. For some reason that made Lois uneasy, all at once she'd wanted him to leave. Her voice had become high and strained. "You'll have to excuse me now. My husband will be home any minute and I need to fix dinner."

"Mrs. Cohen?"

I shifted my focus from the pages to Detective Ellison. "Call me Valentine, please."

"Your first name is really Valentine?"

I grinned. "It's an old family name. Might have started as a spelling mistake on a birth certificate, or just some ancestor's idea of a joke, but my mother insisted on carrying on the tradition."

Detective Ellison pulled her notebook from her jacket pocket. "Tell me what you're getting from the albums."

"A stranger visited Lois in the last few days; he was pretending to be a decorator. But he asked too many questions about her family. At first she liked him but then she became nervous about his manner. She made an excuse and he left."

"Do you think he was the killer?"

"I don't know." I flipped to the last page of photographs. A photo was missing; its outline clearly visible on the page. "But whoever he was, he stole a photograph."

***

The microwave dinged and Jake pulled out the reheated lasagna. Jake could eat anything, any time and be fine. I'd probably have heartburn eating a heavy meal this late, but I didn't have the energy to put something else together.

"Did you talk to anyone?" I put two glasses of iced tea on the table.

He ignored me, wrapping a few garlic rolls in a paper towel and putting them in the microwave.

"Upstairs. Did you see anyone in the house?"

He waited the 30 seconds until the microwave dinged again. "Yes. George Berman is still there. It happened very fast. He doesn't understand why. He's angry and confused. And he's not alone."

"Lois?"

"No. It might be one of the Changs, but whoever it was didn't want to talk to me. Or maybe they were too weak to materialize." Jake stared at the floor, the bundle of bread still in his hand. "George didn't know his killer. Had never seen him before. Male. Light skinned. Tall. There might have been something on his head. A hat or a mask."

"That's all you got?" He'd been upstairs alone almost twenty minutes. I'd danced around Detective Ellison's questions until I'd been dizzy with the effort. Surely he'd gotten more–"

He tossed the hot bread onto the table, one roll escaped and bounced to the tile floor. "Damn it, Valentine. You want me to tell you how much pain he was in? How many times he was stabbed? What his last thoughts were? How he begged for mercy?"

Sometimes I don't like my husband very much. He was going to be eating alone tonight. Maybe sleeping alone too.

***

By morning the snow had stopped completely. The sky was clear, a brilliant blue that was almost too bright to look at. Stamping my feet to clear the snow from my boots, I unlocked the backdoor and entered the kitchen. "Jake, are you up?"

I hadn't seen him before I left at 6 AM to trek down to the local bakery. I had walked down to the shoreline, then doubled back to walk five blocks from our house to the downtown area. The main objective was to clear my head of negative energy and prepare for the stress of another session with the police. My secondary objective was to purchase fresh bagels and a dozen of Jake's favorite cinnamon rolls as a peace offering.

The smell of coffee wafted my way. My husband was awake, even if he wasn't talking to me. "Jake? I've got food."

"He's in the shop–working."

I glanced to my right. My mother-in-law, five-feet, two-inches of pure meanness, was sitting at my kitchen table, my newspaper scattered in front of her. Her favorite blue suit and usual scowl was in place, but her normally gray hair was now inky black. The change was anything but flattering.

"My son has made several sales while you've been out gadding about town. He works too hard."

"Ruth." I tried to choke out more words, something pleasant and friendly, but failed. Ruth had an uncanny ability to find the worst times possible to pop in for a visit. I was serious when I'd told Jake the woman didn't like me; he just refused to face the problem.

"Nice hair," I managed to spit out. "Did you do that yourself?"

"Of course not," Ruth answered, reaching a pale hand up to see if anything had escaped from the well-lacquered beehive style popular in the 1950s. "Hilda did it yesterday afternoon."

"Hilda?"

"Hilda Rosen. She had a shop here in Seamont for forty years before she retired and moved to California."

"And she's back in the hair business?"

"Obviously." She pointed at my hair. "You should pay more attention to your appearance."

Okay, that was probably a fair comment. After all, I hadn't done anything but twist it into a messy braid before I left the house.

"Right." I unpacked my purchases on the kitchen counter. "I'm going to take Jake some breakfast. Do you want–"

I turned back around to face her but she was gone. Probably off to tell Jake again what a poor excuse for a wife he had. I hope she gave him the unabridged version of how unsuitable I am and how in some instances divorce is a wonderful thing.

Smiling, I decided to hold off on taking Jake some rolls. With Ruth in fine form, I might have time to drink a cup of coffee, eat a bagel, and scan the front page of the newspaper before she came back.

***

"Does the man do nothing but stare at the screen all day? Is he trying to put me out of business? Every damn time...."

Good thing nobody was in the shop. Jake was on a tear. I didn't need to be a mind reader or a psychic to know that once again Newton548 had scored something that my husband coveted.

"What was it this time?" I held out the plate with cinnamon rolls.

Jake waved me off and started to pace. He scuttled pass the early 20th century English Arts and Crafts leaded glass mahogany china cabinet which held the collection of Royal Worcester teacups and matching dessert plates which we had picked up a few weeks earlier at an estate sale in Bedford. Husband had died, the wife was moving to Philadelphia to be closer to her daughter. He circled around the Philadelphia Chime Clock which was almost eight feet tall and chimed on the quarter hour and bonged on the hour. It kept perfect time. An old family heirloom of a nice couple in Armonk who were downsizing to a condo in Florida. He finally settled behind the mid-20th century mahogany partners desk that had dovetail constructed drawers on both the front and back, carved legs, and claw and ball feet. We'd picked that up from a couple in Scarsdale. In the midst of a messy divorce, they weren't in the partner mood anymore. Every piece in the crowded shop had a story.

I put the cinnamon rolls on the desk.

"What did the old coot get this time?"

Actually I had no idea if Newton548 was old, a coot, or for that matter, a man or a woman. In the world of on-line antiquing, people can buy and sell anonymously. Jake and I had just gotten in the habit of calling Newton548 a "he."

"An old 1940s radio with bakelite knobs."

"Who's going to buy it?" I looked around the already over-crowded store. "Remember we've got to move most of this stuff into storage or upstairs so the plumbers can work. Maybe we should stop buying until after the new furnace is installed."

"We have plenty of room. Just have to reorganize the large pieces. Create a clear path." Jake reached for a cinnamon bun. He dribbled some crumbs on the desktop and quickly brushed them off. "The radio is in working condition, perfect for the eat-in kitchen at the Bed and Breakfast that Margo is decorating. I sent her a picture of it and she said the owners were thrilled. They're going for this vintage feel to the place. Price was right and I had it. Damn it, I had it when Newton548 swept in and bid like 50 cents above my last price in the final 30 seconds."

A good part of our business was working with decorators looking for one-of-a-kind items. They counted on us, mostly Jake, to know the real from the fake, and to get what they needed at a fair price. We marked up the item to make our profit, the decorator marked it up even more to make her profit. Margo was one of our regulars and I knew Jake would hate to disappoint her.

"Want me to check with the Internet provider again? See if we can get faster upload speed?"

"No." Jake got up and headed for the computer. "I'm going to register a new handle. Newton548 knows I wanted the radio and deliberately bid against me."

I took Jake's place at the desk, picking at the remains of his cinnamon bun. Calories don't count if you are just even-ing out the edges.

Jake's hands flew over the keyboard. "I think he's using my expertise to know what's worth buying and what's not. Probably got his own antique business and saving himself research time. I bet he's got a dozen aliases on eBay, probably acts as a shill for his own auctions. Putting in early bids under different names to drive up the price."

I pushed the plate across the desk. I'd left a smidgen of Jake's cinnamon bun. So all calories consumed were null and void. "Shilling is against the rules on eBay."

He pushed the enter button. "Yeah, well the antique business ain't for the faint of heart. Go big or go home."

"What are you going to tell Margo?"

"That I'll find her another one at the price we agreed on. There's a place in the city that carries those kinds of radios. It will cost us more, but...."

He didn't have to finish the sentence. Margo was a good enough client that it was worth it to cut our profit to keep her happy.

"That's weird." Jake was staring at the computer.

I joined him. He was looking at an ornate antique Chinese Painted Screen with inlaid glass and brass feet. The price was already at $900 and there was more than a day left in the auction.

"Are you thinking of bidding on it? It doesn't look like anything Margo would want. You'd need a pretty big house to–"

Jake shook his head. "I've already owned it once."

"I don't remember it."

"Before I met you." Jake kept staring at the screen. "I recognize it. I wrote up that description a couple of years ago, but took it down when I got a private buyer."

I had no idea what was going on. "Who was the buyer? One of the decorators?

"I sold it to the Changs the week before they were killed. How the hell did Newton548 get a hold of it?"

CHAPTER 6

"Your husband's name is in the Chang murder file," Detective Ellison said, her tone slightly accusing. "Why didn't he tell me? Why didn't you tell me?"

"It's not a secret." I frowned, not happy with how defensive I sounded. "He'd done business with the Changs. And he wasn't my husband then."

She took a sip of tea and waited for me to explain.

I brought over the tea pot and joined her. I really didn't owe her an explanation but Detective Ellison was a good interrogator and obviously had nothing better to do than sit at my kitchen table and eat the last of the cinnamon rolls.

"He'd sold the Changs some antiques a few weeks before the murders. He was questioned by the police along with a dozen other local businessmen. The Changs were remodeling their house, buying new furniture. The last month they were alive there were a string of people going in and out of that house. The Chief made me sit in on all the interviews. Actually she paid me. I was getting $150 an hour just to listen and make notes." I took a sip of tea. "You should let her know that my rates have gone up."

Detective Ellison laughed. "So you met Jake for the first time during one of those interviews? Love at first sight?"

"Not exactly. He had to walk by me a few times." I laughed. More than a few. I'd seen the tall, lanky man with dark troubled eyes walk into the room and known he was hiding something. As I listened to him answer the detectives' questions, I realized he didn't know anything about the Chang murders and whatever secrets he was keeping were personal. I wasn't interested in starting a romantic relationship with anyone at that point in my life, especially a relationship with someone with lots of secrets. I think the only note I made concerned his bad haircut and the fact that the camera in the interview room seemed to make him nervous. Later, after I knew him better, he told me the tiny red light in his peripheral vision kept flickering. He explained some ghosts can't materialize. Sometimes they appear as flickering lights.

"Did you date during the trial?"

I wasn't sure if Detective Ellison was a romantic or was implying some impropriety between a police consultant and a suspect.

"No. Dating came much later. First he saved my life."

***

Detective Ellison paid the delivery boy and set the large pepperoni pizza on my kitchen table, the cinnamon rolls long gone. Shortly after her arrival, she confided that she'd missed both supper the night before and breakfast. As a good hostess, I'd ordered pizza. The detective had insisted on paying. Since I was still slightly annoyed with her from earlier, I let her.

"Do you always get migraines when you have premonitions?"

"No. But I had quite a few during the Fletcher trial." I only put two plates down. Jake was still in the shop, making phone calls, trying to track down where the Chinese screen had been for the last five years. Based on the detective's earlier display of suspicion about his involvement with the Changs, I decided not to mention the antique screen. At least not yet. I had no problem telling her about my vision during the hearing.

"The incident I was telling you about was one of the worst. I was sitting near the back of the crowded courtroom watching Fletcher testify and suddenly I couldn't see. That had never happened before. I'd seen auras before or shadows, but this was total blackness. It was like someone had dropped a bag over my head. Sounds were muffled. I couldn't move my arms. I felt really cold."

Detective Ellison stared at me, a slice of pizza halfway to her open mouth. "What did you do?"

"I didn't know what to do. I must have made some kind of sound. There was pain. It felt like someone was pushing down on the top of my head. I couldn't get any air."

She took a bite, eyes wide, waiting for me to continue.

"Jake was sitting in the row behind me. I hadn't noticed him. Later he told me he'd been coming to the trial regularly to watch me." I chuckled. "My own personal stalker."

"This where you tell me how he saved you?"

I nodded. "He'd known something was wrong and managed to walk me out of there without anyone realizing I was acting strangely. Ten minutes later, just as I'd been about to allow him to take me to the emergency room, the episode was over. A few days later, I was fired and he showed up at my apartment with flowers and a bottle of wine."

That was the abbreviated version of our courtship. Detective Ellison had no need to hear about how badly my world had fallen apart after the Chief had thrown me to the media wolves.

Detective Ellison took another slice of pizza. While she sprinkled parmesan cheese on top, she asked me something no one, not even Jake, had ever asked. "The episode or whatever that happened in the courtroom. You said it was a premonition. A premonition of what?"

She looked up, shaker in hand waiting expectantly.

I shook my head. I didn't have an answer for her.

***

Later that evening I found my husband stretched out on the sofa in the den. He was eating leftover pizza, scattering crumbs on the upholstery. Since the sofa was Ruth's I wasn't too upset. He could deal with his mother.

"Why aren't you moving furniture? It's not going to move itself."

He made a sound that indicated he heard me but wasn't going to bother answering.

Jake, what are you doing?" I lifted his feet and sat down next to him. He put his feet in my lap and wiggled his sock-clad toes. Humoring him, I started rubbing them.

"Watching a basketball game." He grinned. "I have money on it."

"I should have told Diane about Newton548 and the Chinese screen."

"Diane?"

"Detective Ellison."

"Now she's Diane?"

I wasn't surprised at his expression of disbelief. I didn't have that many friends. I didn't have any friends that were cops. "We bonded over the pizza you're eating."

"Right." He shook his head. "Well, there's nothing to tell your friend Diane yet. While you were bonding did you ask her what happened to the Changs' possessions?"

"Yes." I rubbed my knuckles back and forth over his arches. "She said the Changs' daughter took a few family heirlooms, mementos, photos, that sort of thing. Otherwise everything sold with the house. The Bermans bought the house and contents. From what I saw the other day, the Bermans didn't keep much of the furniture."

"Who handled the sale of the house?"

"She didn't say. I figured with your vast contacts you could find that out." I smiled and squeezed his toes one more time. "Tomorrow will be soon enough. I want your undivided attention tonight."

"Yes, ma'am." He shifted his feet off my lap, sat up, and motioned for me to move by his side. I put my head on his shoulder, enjoying the comfort of his body.

"Did you turn the furnace off? Or did it just stop? It's cold in here." I burrowed deeper into the sofa back, nestling between him and the cushions. "We should start a fire in the fireplace."

"Too much trouble. I'll keep you warm."

"I might need a sweater too." I smiled, then brushed my lips over his. "How much did you want to watch the basketball game?"

"I could be persuaded to check the score later." He pulled my hair free from the clip I'd used after my shower. "Here's a question, Val. Why did it take so long to sell the Chang house? It was almost five years after the Changs died before the Bermans purchased it."

"I actually know the answer to that one." I kissed him again, this time tasting the pizza before I pulled away.

"You're a tease," he said, hugging me with both arms. "Tell me."

"Diane said that the Chang daughter wanted a quick sale to get the money for her kid's college tuition. That didn't happen. Besides the house being considered a crime scene for months, the Changs failed to leave a will. A couple of distant relatives made claims. The estate was tied up in litigation for almost two years, then when that was finally settled, there was the small problem of the house's reputation. Bermans got the house and contents for $40,000 under asking. It was a real steal."

Jake sighed, resting his chin on the top of my head. "Yeah, they got a real bargain."

***

The same premonition came as a dream.

The child was standing on the windowsill. He was wearing a dishcloth cape again. This time I knew the child was a boy. He was young, not old enough to be in school. He was looking at a tree limb located at least ten feet below, his right hand was outstretched.

"What's your name?" I tried to get his attention but he paid me no attention.

A door slammed in his room. The child glanced behind him, then jumped.

I screamed.

Or at least I screamed in my dream. I jerked awake, sitting up and trying to get my bearings. Jake was still asleep next to me. The only sound in the dark, cold room was the ticking of the antique alarm clock and the wind outside. I squinted at the hands on the clock. 3 AM. Nothing good ever happened at 3 AM.

Shivering, I padded to the bureau and pulled out one of Jake's sweatshirts and a pair of his thick athletic socks over my thin nightgown. Dressing quickly, I was headed back to bed when our bedroom window rattled. Sitting down on the window seat I stared out into the snowy night. We'd probably have another six inches of snow on the ground before daybreak.

I could hear the clock ticking and realized that it was past time. I was going to be late. "Valentine?"

I opened my eyes and found myself back in bed, Jake held out a cup of coffee. As I sat up to take it I discovered I was still in my nightgown. I knew without looking that the old fashioned alarm clock of the night before had been replaced by a digital one with flashing red numbers.

"You okay?"

I smiled and pulled the blankets up. No use telling him that time was getting away from us.

CHAPTER 7

A telephone call from one of our regular customers delayed my plans to relocate inventory from the shop to other parts of the house. Besides the plumbers and their need for space, we had to make room for some expected shipments. But instead, I had to spend almost two hours on-line bidding on a dining room set. One of our clients had gotten news of the sale at the last minute and needed us to close the deal.

Jake was better at bidding strategy than I was. I tended to place my bids too quickly. As Jake had told me over and over, running down the clock could save a lot of money. Me, I was always more afraid of losing.

Speaking of losing, Newton548 hadn't placed a bid. Either he wasn't in the mood for Chippendale or he'd been unaware of the sale. His absence meant I was able to win the auction for about $500 under budget.

I had just finalized the payment when Jake called, he was on his way back, delivery made, and now food was on his to-do list. He wanted to know if Chinese was okay for a late lunch. He had a craving.

Over hot and sour soup, Szechuan shrimp, and fried rice, I found out that Jake had rearranged my afternoon.

I looked down at the empty takeout boxes and sighed. "So this was a bribe?"

"Absolutely."

"Is it going to involve me putting on shoes and makeup?"

He glanced at my fuzzy slippers. "Makeup is optional."

***

Three hours and sixty miles later, I was home again. Against Jake's advice I'd taken my eight-year-old Volkswagen bug convertible since the snowplows had cleared the roads of the worst of the snow and ice. I shouldn't have, it was still too cold even with the top up. As Jake reminded me, it wasn't a practical car for New York winters. More than once, he'd mentioned selling it and getting me something sturdier. But the bug predated my marriage and was one of the few things I had left that was mine. When I'd married Jake, I'd moved into his family home, I'd joined his business, heck, I was sleeping on his mother's sheets, but the bug was mine, all mine. It was paid for, got great gas mileage, and I loved driving it. Most of the time.

"Not there."

Jake didn't even look up from his computer. He waved in the direction of the storeroom.

"You want the Limoges china service in there?" I'd just come from buying a service for 16 from an estate sale in Bedford, along with the buffet that had held it. I'd cleared a space in the western corner of the shop before I'd left. I'd done all that work, mind you, by myself because Jake was at the bank getting the details on refinancing our mortgage. I'd done the heavy lifting and now he was overruling me. Some partnership.

I stopped just short of stamping my foot. "Why?"

Silence. Jake was hunched over his laptop, hand hovering over the touchpad.

"Where do you want this?"

Zeke Harrison, who handled all our furniture deliveries, stood in the doorway, cold air blasting into the shop. He had met me in Bedford with his truck in order to transport all my purchases.

"Zeke, I want it in that corner, but apparently Mr. Cohen here has another opinion."

Sarcasm was lost on my husband who suddenly was typing furiously and then virtually punching the touchpad to enter the data.

Jake mumbled, "It's the last two minutes of the auction. I'll be damned if Newton548 is getting the World's Fair desk calendar. No way."

He looked up briefly from his laptop vigil. "Why's it colder than usual in here?"

"Sorry, Mr. Cohen."

Zeke moved into the shop and closed the door behind him. "Where do you want the china and buffet?"

I'd met Zeke Harrison after I married Jake. He was football tackle kind of big, but could move the most delicate china and crystal without so much as a scratch. He had a small crew of three equally muscled, but gentle brutes. Over 10 years, he'd built up a niche trucking business which handled the deliveries for most of the serious antique dealers in the tri-state area. All that time handling estate sales had also given him a well-trained eye. He'd waved me off a couple of times at estate sales when he thought the price for an item was too high.

Question forgotten, Jake was back hovering over the touchpad, so an executive decision had to be made. "I've cleared a spot in that corner."

"Maybe we should wait for Mr. Cohen." Zeke was nothing if not practical. He wasn't about to move it twice. "What's he bidding on?"

I glanced over to the laptop. "A 1939 New York World's Fair Perpetual Calendar."

"Mint condition," Jake muttered.

Zeke looked around the shop. "Mr. Cohen sell the memorabilia? I don't see anything...."

I shook my head. "Sometimes he does. Mostly at the collector shows. He's got some of the more expensive items on display in our living room, others are packed and ready for the show in a couple of months."

"Yes," Jake gave a fist pump like he'd just won a marathon. "That'll show him. Slid right in there in the last 30 seconds and outbid him."

He pushed back from the counter. "Hey, Zeke. Thanks for helping us out."

Zeke nodded. "No problem. Who's the big enemy?"

Jake laughed. "Some bozo named Newton548. Always seems to be watching what I'm buying and then sandbagging me in the last minute."

"Where's he from?"

Jake shook his head. "No clue. Although I think he's a dealer too. Okay, let's get the show on the road."

"On the road to where?" I was getting impatient. "Where do you want all of it?"

Jake looked slowly around the shop. "How about you put the buffet in that corner. Seems kind of empty. Val, maybe you can put some of the china on display on top?"

I gave him my best death ray glare but it didn't work; he was still standing. He didn't seem to be reading my thoughts, so I had to spell it out for him. "You mean the corner that I emptied four hours ago?"

Jake grinned. "Yeah, that one."

CHAPTER 8

"Val? Are you up here again? Are we taking a break and you didn't tell me?"

I was sitting on a floral settee in a large bedroom on the third floor. Jake's paternal grandparents had used this bedroom for fifty years. We had more bedrooms than we needed on the lower floors, so we didn't use this one. Jake's mother hadn't cared much for her in-laws so she rarely ventured in here. Jake usually never made it to the third floor. As far as I knew the room was furnished much the same as it was when Jake's grandparents had been alive. After I had moved into the house, I'd made it my refuge. It was quiet and the light was wonderful in the morning.

"I thought so," Jake said, pushing open the half-closed door. "You can't hide from me in here. What is it about you and this room?"

I smiled. "I like visiting with your grandparents."

He laughed and sat down beside me. "They're not here. Believe me I'd know it if they were."

I leaned into him. "Some of their memories still are. They loved you very much."

"I played on that rug over there," Jake said, pointing towards an area rug in front of a fireplace. "I loved miniature cars. I'd pretend the pattern in the rug was a road. While I pushed the cars back and forth, my grandfather would read to me."

"Your grandmother's dresser still has her things inside. Her lingerie. Her makeup. No one ever packed up her things? Your father?"

"No, my father couldn't. My grandfather wouldn't." Jake slipped his hand into mine. "My grandfather was like me, you know. He fought hard to hang onto what and who he loved."

I gazed into his hazel eyes and considered what he was trying to say. "It's hard to imagine living with someone that long, then being without them."

Jake shook his head. "He wasn't without her. My grandmother died five years before my grandfather did, but they left this house together."

"You, Jake Cohen, are a romantic." I gave him a quick kiss.

He hugged me, then grinned. "I'm also a great detective. I've tracked him down."

"Who?" It took me a couple of seconds. "No, you didn't?"

His eyes sparkled with excitement. "Yep. Newton548. Want to take a drive?"

***

"Okay Sherlock, how did you find him?"

We were on the Bronx River Parkway heading to Mt. Vernon.

"Elementary Watson," Jake switched lanes, finally passing an Oldsmobile Cutlass spewing smoke from its ancient muffler. "I bought a Chinese urn he was selling. Looks a lot like the one I'd sold to the Changs before they were killed. Offered to pick it up rather than risk shipping."

"But how did you know he was even in the New York area?"

Jake took his eyes off the road long enough to give me a withering look. Like I should have been able to connect the dots. The proverbial lightbulb went off.

"You bought something else from him that he shipped and the address...."

Jake smiled. "I knew you'd catch up sooner or later. The address was for one of those mailbox rental services, but the postmark...."

I hate when he's smug.

"And your plan is to ask him where he got the Chang merchandise? And then what?"

Jake exited the parkway and headed south on Lincoln Avenue. "Not sure. Maybe he'll be willing to tell me his source, maybe I'll just beat the crap out of him."

I laughed. Jake is many things, but a fighter he's not. "You're talking figuratively, right?"

He pulled into a parking spot in front of a row of apartment buildings. A small coffee shop anchored the corner. "This is it."

"Which one is his building?"

"Don't know. He agreed to meet me at Theresa's Luncheonette."

Theresa hadn't put much money into decorating or for that matter, cleaning supplies. The counter and stools dated from the 1950s and I was pretty sure that so did the grease. We were the only ones in the place, other than the help.

Jake picked up the menu. "Hey, did you see she's got homemade cannoli?"

The man has an iron stomach.

The waitress who was at least 60, or maybe just a hard 40, tapped her order pad. Jake smiled and the waitress, like most women, smiled back at my good-looking husband.

"Coffee and a cannoli, please. Val, what do you want?"

"Do you have any bottled water?"

The waitress nodded toward a small refrigerated case in the corner.

I sipped my water and listened to Jake's excited cries of delight over the creaminess of the cannoli. He finished his coffee and asked for a refill.

We'd been there 15 minutes and no one had come in, not even to buy a lottery ticket and the jackpot was over $3 million.

"How long are we going to wait?"

The waitress slapped the check on the counter.

"Excuse me, Miss." Jake was always polite. "Do you know someone named Newton who I think lives around here?"

The waitress shook her head. "Never heard of him. Hey, Theresa, do you know anybody with the name...What did you say?"

"Newton. Goes by the online name Newton548."

We all looked at the woman behind the cash register. "Nah, nobody around here with that name. Only Newton I know is a street."

Jake and I exchanged glances. "How far away is it? Can we walk it?"

Theresa nodded. "Go down Havelin two blocks, turn right on Newton."

Jake slammed a $20 bill on the counter. "Thanks and the cannoli was great."

We hustled out of the luncheonette. I grabbed hold of Jake's sleeve. "Wait a minute. You don't even know if that's an address or the person just loves *Fig Newtons*."

Jake gave me another withering look. "You're right. But it's worth investigating. You coming with me or want to wait here. You really ought to try the cannoli."

I sniffed. "Don't need the calories. Let's go."

Luck was on our side. Newton Street was a one-way thoroughfare and the first house number was 540. Four houses later we stood in front of a small Colonial with peeling paint, overgrown weeds, and dead bushes. The other houses on the street were well-maintained. If this really was Newton548 of online repute, he clearly wasn't putting any money into his living quarters.

We carefully picked our way down the broken concrete path that led to the front porch. The place made the Bates Motel look like the Ritz.

"I've got a bad feeling about this," I whispered.

Jake stopped. "A premonition?"

I shook my head. "No, common sense. This place is a dump."

Jake stepped up to the porch and rang the bell. He waited a moment, then knocked on the door. As if in a very bad movie, it swung open to reveal a small entry foyer, piled with newspapers and trash.

I took a step back and pulled on Jake's sleeve. "Come on, something's wrong."

Jake seemed transfixed, staring straight ahead. Sweat was starting to bead on his forehead. I could hear short gasps, like he was trying to catch his breath.

I turned his face to me. "Jake, what is it?"

Finally, in a voice barely a whisper, "He's dead."

"How do you know that?" I looked in the foyer. There was nothing there but garbage.

"Because his ghost just told me so. Newton548 has been murdered."

***

I pulled out my phone to dial 9-1-1, but Jake shook his head.

"We've got to call the police," I whispered. "The killer could still be in there. Maybe Newton548 is alive."

Jake pulled me down the front walk. "The killer is gone, long gone. And Newton548 is definitely dead. I've got to think."

We walked quickly back to the car. Once settled, I handed him a half-filled bottle of water that I found on the backseat. I remembered drinking it several days earlier. It was the best I could do. He took a swig, then poured some on his handkerchief and wiped his face with it.

When his color was better, I started again. "We've got to call the cops. We can't just leave him there."

"And what are you going to say to the cops in Mount Vernon. My husband talks to ghosts and he said there's a dead body at 548 Newton?"

"So we call the Seamont police. They know us...."

Jake shook his head. "They know you, not me, and the Chief thinks you're a flake."

"Excuse me?"

Jake shrugged. "The Chief thinks you're crazy, but she doesn't know me. I want to keep it that way."

He gave a small smile and I couldn't decide if I was happy that he could joke or furious that he would joke about me.

Jake took a deep breath, maybe to clear his mind of what he'd just seen. "Okay, call your friend Diane and ask her to meet us at *our* house. It's going to take some explaining and it's probably better done in person."

Detective Ellison wasn't on duty, but I left a message with the desk sergeant. I said it was urgent that we talk. He recognized my name and said he'd pass along the info.

"Jake, you okay to drive?"

He looked better, but still shaken.

"No problem. Let's go."

He drove slower than usual. I started to turn on the radio, but he put his hand over mine. I probably should have given him some space, but I had questions I wanted answered before we met Diane.

"Who killed him?"

Jake took a moment before he spoke. "He didn't know his killer. Newton548 was an old man. Killer knocked him down, then held a knife to his throat."

He shuddered. He was reliving the scene as if he were there in real time. I put my hand on his shoulder to bring him back to me.

"Maybe it was just a break-in. Nothing to do with this mess."

Jake checked his side mirror and then moved into the left lane. "Newton548 kept saying he didn't have it anymore. The killer wanted something and Newton548 didn't have it. The old man had sold it."

"What is it? What's the killer looking for? Who did Newton548 sell it to?"

Jake stopped the car at a red light and took the moment to glare at me. "I don't get a transcript, Val. Sometimes I only see glimpses of what happened. That's why I don't want to work with the cops. They're looking for precise answers and I don't have them. They wouldn't believe me. They'd think I was holding out on them. I'll be lucky if they didn't think I'm the killer or at least working with him."

The car behind us honked. The light had turned green.

I felt horrid. I better than anyone knew what it's like to have no one believe you. I wallowed in a little self-pity while Jake focused on his driving.

His voice interrupted my pity party. "We've got to find the buyer."

"How? For that matter, why?"

Jake pulled into our driveway. "I've got no idea how, but so far 5 people are dead because the killer wants something. Whoever bought it is the next victim."

Detective Ellison pulled in behind us. We still hadn't come up with a plan for how to explain the dead body in Mt. Vernon. But we were racing the clock to find the next intended victim.

***

"Interesting." Detective Ellison scribbled something else in her notebook. "Newton548. You don't have a name?"

I glanced at Jake. He was pacing back and forth across the kitchen, letting me give Diane the news. "No."

"And you just woke up this morning knowing that he...this Newton person was dead? Like from a dream?"

"Yeah, but not just dead. Murdered."

"Right." She flipped back a page. "Murdered. Stabbed. Got it. Anything else?"

"You…you didn't say stabbed when you first told me." Jake said in a soft, insistent voice.

I was confused. I knew he'd mentioned a knife when we were at the victim's house.

I tried to cover, but it sounded fake even to me. "I'm sorry. I'm a little overwhelmed and sometimes I get mixed up." I wiped my eyes, as if tears were threatening to fall.

Jake needed to tell his story, even if he was going to pretend it was mine. But all he'd done was pace the length and width of the Oriental rug in the living room, so far four times.

Didn't much matter. It was painfully obvious that Detective Ellison...uh Diane didn't believe a word of what I'd told her. Which, upon reflection, kind of pissed me off. She had no way of knowing that I was lying. She and Hardesty came to me, asking for my help. Now that I was giving it to her, she was acting like I was making it all up. And I was, but the point is, she didn't know that.

Jake, sensing I was about to pitch a fit, decided to join the conversation.

"So will you check it out? Or get the Mt. Vernon police to–"

Detective Ellison looked from Jake back to me. "I'll ask them to do a wellness check. But I'll tell you this, if they find a body, that dream story isn't going to work.

Now's the time for you to tell me if you know more about this than you're saying. Where were you this morning?"

"This morning?" I was stalling. Obviously, the detective was laying a trap for me.

She smiled. I thought it looked more predatory than amused.

"You've already been to Mt. Vernon, haven't you? You found a body?"

Jake caved first. "We drove over there, but we didn't go inside. That's the truth."

There must have been something on his face that the detective believed. "I'll call it in."

I flounced out of the room without further comment. I was upset with her attitude and I didn't care if she knew it. She should have trusted me. Obviously I'd overestimated the depth of our three-day friendship!

***

"Did she say she would call?" I asked stripping off the rubber gloves I'd been using.

Jake was working on inventory in the shop. I'd done two loads of laundry and scrubbed down two bathrooms in my zeal to capitalize on the energy spurt brought on by my righteous anger.

"She did."

"She said she would call? It's been four hours. When do you think we'll hear something?"

Jake looked up from his paperwork. He looked haggard and sad.

"She called about a half hour ago."

Well, hell. I waited, but he didn't continue. I felt like I was talking to a truculent teenager, refusing to share what he knew, parsing every word he uttered.

"Did they find the body? Any fingerprints? What did she say for crying out loud?"

Jake's voice was so low I could barely hear him. "That Stan Freedman, aka Newton548, died of natural causes."

I slid into an antique rocking chair. "I thought his ghost said he'd been murdered."

Jake's face twisted in pain, like he was reliving the scene in real time. "He did. He was."

"But who stabs himself to death? He slit his own throat?"

Jake shook his head. "I never said that. I said, or actually Newton said, that the killer held a knife to his throat."

"So how did he die?"

"An overdose of Sorbitrate."

"What's that?"

"Drug used for angina. He was holding a prescription bottle in his hand when he died. Very helpful if used correctly, deadly if not. Killer had Newton swallow extra pills. Probably didn't help Newton's heart that he was scared to death, literally."

Jake gave a small laugh. The kind you make when you're trying not to cry.

I tried to bring him back to reality. "Okay, so he was forced to overdose. Isn't that murder?"

Jake shook his head. "Not when Franklin Freedman, Newton's great-nephew and his emergency contact, says that Stan was old, getting senile, and it was no surprise that he overdosed. Nephew insisted that the family had tried to put the old coot into a nursing home, but he refused to go. "

"So tell Diane what you know."

Jake laughed again. And this time, he sounded like he actually found the idea funny. "Right. Excuse me Ms. Detective. I've got an exclusive, direct from Stan Freedman's ghost. He assured me that appearances to the contrary, he was murdered."

Jake started talking in a falsetto. "Really Mr. Cohen. Did the ghost tell you who his killer was?"

"Nope. Said he didn't know him."

Resuming his very bad Diane imitation, he continued. "So did he say why he was killed?"

"No, he didn't. Just that he didn't have what the killer wanted."

Once again faux Diane appeared. "And what was that, Mr. Cohen? What did the killer want?"

"Oops. Sorry, I don't have a clue what the killer wanted."

Jake looked me in the eyes. "Think she'll buy it?"

I think I preferred broken-hearted Jake to sarcastic one. I took a deep breath and tried another tact.

"Did you tell her about the items you purchased from him? About the Chinese screen having belonged to the Changs?"

He nodded. "She doesn't think it's connected. Said the Chang items have probably been bought and sold many times."

"Do you?" I ran my hands down the polished arms of the rocker. The wood was beautiful. I rocked a little, absorbing a sensation of peace and calm. The former owner of the chair had been happy. Her name was Laura. She'd lived a long life with lots of family surrounding her.

"No, Val. I don't know why exactly, but I would like to see what Newton548 sold since the Changs were murdered. See if he'd acquired more of the items I'd sold to the Changs."

"What if Newton548 lied to his killer? What if he had no idea what the killer wanted and he just told him he'd sold it to buy some time? Or maybe he did know but wanted to keep it. Or maybe he sold it, but hadn't delivered it. Maybe he tried to bluff the killer. Maybe Newton548 still has it. We should search his house."

"Search it for what? No." Jake held up one hand. "Valentine, I promised your best buddy Diane that in the future we would let her do all the field work. We are supposed to call her if we get another clue."

I shrugged and rocked a little faster. "We're not that close any more."

CHAPTER 9

She came up behind me, startling me. One minute I was all alone and the next she was there, invading my space. Sometimes my psychic abilities fail me when I need them the most.

"I can't believe you have my son eating bacon. You know he has to watch his cholesterol."

Ruth's was just the voice I wanted to hear the first thing in the morning. I was fixing breakfast. My mother-in-law had not been invited to join us for the meal.

"The bacon is for me." It was. Mostly. Okay, my husband had been known to steal a slice or two when I wasn't looking.

"Why are you frying four slices? Tell me that Ms. Zalmanzig."

I didn't bother turning to face her. She refused to treat me with respect, but for Jake's sake I tried to maintain the peace or at least avoid open warfare.

I turned the bacon. "I'm hungry, Ruth. And my last name is the same as yours now. It's been four years. When are you going to accept our marriage?"

"When am I going to get grandchildren?"

Instead of answering her, I countered with, "Are you staying for breakfast? Should I set three plates?"

"I would rather have my teeth drilled."

An image of her in a dentist's chair flashed in my mind. I bet the dentist was the one who insisted on her getting gas.

"I could fix you an omelet?"

The sound of her heels clicking on the back staircase ended our impromptu visit. Jake's mother had accomplished her mission for the day, I felt both inadequate and perhaps a little guilty over dangling pork in front of Ruth's perfect son.

The telephone rang and I continued to ponder the mystery of families, especially mothers. They were both a comfort and a burden. Even from 1000 miles away.

I removed the crispy bacon from the pan, wiped my hands on a paper towel, and then grabbed the phone, punching the speaker phone option.

I didn't need to see the phone number to know who was calling. I wasn't the only female in my family to have a sixth sense. "Hi Momma."

"Valentine? You need to stand up to that woman."

"Good morning to you too. Yes, I know, but Jake loves her so I try to keep the peace. But it's not easy."

"I've got a good mind to come up there and deal with her once and for all. I knew at the wedding she was going to be a problem for you. Didn't I tell you?"

"Yes, Momma. Hey, you're up early. More trouble with Aunt Sarah?" I cracked three eggs in a bowl. Jake liked his eggs scrambled with a little bit of chopped onion.

"No more than usual. Honey, do you remember Joey Burk? A nice boy. He's a doctor now. Such a shame you broke up with him. His mother is a saint! I play bingo with her every week at the church. You should apologize to Joey for whatever you did back then. His mother said he's still single."

"I'm not apologizing. He's the one who said I was crazy and dumped me right before the prom. Momma, we were in the ninth grade when...." I couldn't help laughing. My "Joey" phase had been mercifully short but tragic in a way that only a shy teenager could fully appreciate. "I think we've both moved on. Plus now I have Jake. He might not be a doctor but he's cute."

"I suppose. What would I know since I never get to see you two."

I laughed again. My mother loved Jake. But she'd love him a lot more if he'd agree to relocate to Oklahoma. "We can't get away right now because of the shop. But you and Aunt Sarah are always welcome to visit."

"Your aunt and I aren't exactly speaking at the moment. She had the nerve to–"

Beating the eggs a little faster, I changed the subject. "Have you talked to Aunt Delia? Has she gotten over the trauma of Allison and Peter's elopement?"

***

Gazing in my closet I chose the navy blue wool suit that made me look like a corporate lawyer. I had a meeting with Chief Liza Peterson. Our first meeting was cancelled when Jake and I had gone after the carjacker and kidnapped baby. Chief Peterson had grudging accepted that excuse, but I was left with the distinct impression that another absence would have dire consequences. I wasn't sure what she could do to me, but I didn't want to find out. I might have forgotten to pay a couple of parking tickets.

Dressing quickly before I lost my nerve, I walked over and checked out my image in the full-length mirror standing in the corner of our bedroom. The pencil skirt with the little kick pleat did great things for my legs. The jacket was just long enough to hide anything extra I might be carrying around my hips. I had a v-neck sweater to wear underneath it. Black pumps and tiny pearl earrings completed the look. I'd already braided my hair and pinned it up. It would probably stay that way for about two hours before gravity took hold and strands started escaping. But for now it looked good and if the meeting lasted more than two hours, my hair wouldn't be the only part of me planning an escape.

***

"Ms. Zalmanzig, please have a seat."

I frowned. Chief Peterson knew my married name. She was trying to irritate me, put me on the defensive. Not for the first time I wondered why she thought she could ask for my help in one breath and then insult me with the next.

Counting to ten, I walked slowly over to the chair parked in front of the police chief's desk. I noted the desk was piled with papers and files, an outdated computer almost buried under the mess. I took a good look at the woman. She was in full uniform but still managed to look unkempt. There were circles under her eyes and lines on her face that weren't there earlier in the year when she'd given an interview to a local TV station.

"Please, call me Mrs. Cohen," I said, lowering myself into the chair and crossing my legs.

The Chief nodded, a flicker of respect shone in her gaze. Or maybe I was just projecting what I wanted to see.

"Detective Ellison tells me you've come up with some new leads in the Berman case."

"And in the Chang case," I added. I wasn't above tossing a little salt in the wound. The woman had used and abused me five years earlier, ignoring me when I told her she'd arrested the wrong man, and negating the value of my work in her interviews with the press about the Chang murders.

"Yes, well...." Chief Peterson leaned one ample hip on her desk and stared down at me. "Perhaps there is a connection between the two cases. Alex Fletcher may have enlisted an accomplice to kill the Bermans in order to influence his latest appeal of his conviction. Has his lawyer contacted you yet?"

My former friend Diane hadn't mentioned anything about an appeal. I tried to remember her exact words when she and Detective Hardesty had shown up in the shop and requested my assistance. It was a little fuzzy. I had focused on the information about the murder and the Chief's apology. Although thinking back, I'm not sure if Diane had relayed an apology. I distinctly remember that she said that the Chief knew she had been wrong and needed my help. Sitting in the Chief's office now, I wasn't picking up any "I was wrong, forgive me" vibe from the woman. I was beginning to think my former friend Diane had lied to me for her own purposes. Or perhaps Chief Peterson had changed her mind yet again.

"Ms. Zalmanzig? Did you hear what I said?"

"Cohen. Mrs. Cohen." I reined in my thoughts and concentrated on answering the Chief's original question. "I have not been contacted by anyone in connection with the Chang and Berman murders except your detectives. They offered me a job. They claimed to be acting on your behalf."

"A job? There's no money for that even if I wanted...." Chief Peterson frowned. "I asked them to interview you, determine if you had any connection to the Bermans, before Fletcher's attorneys got to you. Son of a bitch is guilty as hell."

I had no desire to argue with her. The woman hadn't changed a bit in five years. "Your detectives were supposed to be eliminating me as a suspect?"

"You and your husband."

"You're certifiable. I'm done trying to help you." I uncrossed my legs and prepared to stand up. I hadn't needed to worry about my hair. This meeting wasn't going to take any time at all.

"Hold on," Chief Peterson said, motioning for me to stay put. "I'll have a talk with Ellison and Hardesty about their methods, but since you're here, we might as well discuss your theory."

If I hadn't been worried that someone else was going to get killed before Liza Peterson pulled her head out of her ass, I would have walked out of that office without saying another word. Instead I took a deep breath and told her everything. Or at least everything she needed to know.

***

The ladies room at the police station wasn't going to win any awards. I did my business quickly. I spared a few minutes in front of a cracked mirror, trying to repair my hairstyle and thinking over the discussion I'd had with Chief Peterson.

I was a little chagrined that I'd fallen so easily for Detectives Ellison and Hardesty's manipulations. They had sensed what it would take to get my cooperation and given it to me. I was left wondering what they had expected to happen when I found out, or if they'd even care. In their eyes, Jake and I could easily have been involved in the killings. I was only assuming that we'd been cleared or Chief Peterson wouldn't have called me in for a meeting. She wanted me to watch the police interviews with the Berman daughters. I'd agreed, reluctantly.

"Wimp," I said to the woman in the mirror. "You should have told her *no* and walked out."

I finished rebraiding my hair just as the door opened and two women entered. From their appearance I was guessing they were civilians. When I got a good look at one of the women's faces I recognized Trish. She was exactly as she'd been in the photo I'd seen in the Berman house. The other woman was a few years older, her frosted blonde hair cut short. Claudia. I think that's what Lois Berman had told the stranger. I wouldn't have recognized her without her sister's presence. She wasn't aging well.

The counter held six sinks, so there was plenty of room for them to join me there. I played with my hair a little more, stalling for time. They spared me a glance or two, but were engrossed in a conversation about why Beth, their youngest sibling, had been named executor of their parents' estate. Neither thought it was a good idea since Beth was in California and they were both living in Boston. They had expected to be able to collect some of their mother's things during this trip. Their lawyer had said that wasn't possible. The police had echoed that opinion. The sisters weren't happy.

Claudia dropped a lipstick and it rolled on the tiled floor towards me.

I leaned over and picked it up. A scene flashed in front of my eyes. Claudia arguing with a teenaged girl.

"Where were you last night?"

"I told you. Cara and I were studying at–"

"I know what you said. You lie to me again and you'll be grounded until you're twenty-one."

"Alright, we were at a club okay."

"Someone broke into this house; they knew the alarm codes. Where was your boyfriend? Where was Toby?"

"Mom! I can't believe you....You've never liked him. Toby wasn't even in town."

"He can tell the police all about it. They are going to be paying him a visit."

"You told the police Toby did it? I can't believe you did that. He's never going to speak to me again."

"Good."

I handed the lipstick back to her and left feeling uncomfortable about invading her privacy. I never knew when I was going to get a "read" from touching an item or a person. There didn't seem to be any rhyme or reason to it.

If Claudia dropped the same lipstick again and I picked it up, I might get nothing at all.

Despite how I got the information, the mention of the break-in at Claudia's house couldn't be ignored. Was there a connection to her parents' murders? It would be interesting to know when Claudia's house was robbed and whether it was before or after her parents were killed.

***

"When was the last time you saw your parents?"

Claudia took a drink of water before answering. "Just a week or so after they moved into the new house. They gave me some furniture for my den and I had to make arrangements to have it shipped. We used someone local. Cost me an arm and a leg."

"Did they mention anything about threats? Did they have any enemies?"

I was sitting behind a two-way mirror, listening to the interview on ancient speakers hanging from the wall. The small, darkened room smelled of cigarettes and unwashed laundry. I wouldn't want to spend much time in there.

Detective Ellison was asking most of the questions. As usual Detective Hardesty was sitting back and letting his partner take the lead while he made notes and observed. I hadn't seen him in a couple of days. He'd shaved off the beard he'd been working on. His appearance was much improved. The thought that he'd been working undercover entered my mind. Something to do with gangs. He was favoring one shoulder. Something was wrong with it.

The door opened and Chief Peterson joined me. She sat down on a metal folding chair next to me. "Anything?"

"I don't think Claudia is lying, if that's what you mean." I'd already mentioned Claudia's house break-in to the Chief. She said she'd look into it, but I had my doubts. "The woman is stressed, but that's to be expected with her parents' murder and raising a teenager."

Chief Peterson sighed. "Her sister is waiting in the other interview room. I'm not psychic but neither look good for the murders."

"I agree. Unless you insist, I'm not going to stay. See if you can get a list of what her parents gave her that last visit. Also a list of anything that was—"

"Yeah, yeah," Chief Peterson stood. "I know. You want to know if anything that was stolen was something the Changs had owned. Frankly I think that's a dead end too. Will probably end up being a stunt Claudia's daughter and her boyfriend pulled to get some ready cash."

I gave up. There was only so much I could tell someone who refused to hear. As I left the police station my mind was on shopping for dinner and picking up the dry cleaning before the shop closed. One look at the bug and I knew neither was happening.

My back right tire was flat.

CHAPTER 10

The television weatherman was predicting unseasonably cold temperatures for the next week. Great, just great. I hope we didn't end up with frozen pipes before the furnace was replaced.

"The tire is ruined," Jake said, adding more cheerful news to my morning. "Mickey at the garage asked if we had any enemies. He said someone took a knife to it."

I stopped pouring cereal and turned to look at my husband. "I was parked in the police station parking lot. I can't believe someone would be crazy enough to...there were people going in and out...it wasn't even dark outside."

"Probably kids." He ignored my protests and put two slices of toast in the toaster. "I don't want you driving without a spare, not in this weather. I'll take it into the garage today after I deliver that china set to the auction house."

"Kids? Come on! Don't you think someone was trying to send us a message? It's no secret that we've been working with the police on the Berman murders." I closed the cereal box and considered the situation. Were we being watched and I hadn't noticed? I should have sensed something.

"Val, if that was a message it was unnecessary. You said yourself that the police have been lying to us. Why should you continue trying to help them? There are plenty of things here we should be focusing on. The furnace repairs for one thing. It's going to make a serious dent in our savings. Not to mention the disruption to our business. Did you see that latest estimate from Javier? We need to finish moving the merchandise so his crew can get in and out tomorrow. Can you just concentrate on the shop today and let the police do their own work? Please?"

"I can try." He didn't seem to notice the sarcasm in my tone.

I handed him a bowl of cereal and we ate a quick breakfast standing at the kitchen island. The man was forgetting that I hadn't asked to be involved in the police investigation. I was afraid that the slashed tire might mean that I still had no control over where this was all going.

***

We were in a race against time, if Javier Baez was correct. At some point, the oil tank was going to do more than leak and then what a mess. Jake was right. We needed to get to work on the relocation of the furniture and memorabilia that stood between us and reliable heat.

So I was in the process of moving the breakable items from the shop to our living quarters. Who was I kidding? Everything in the shop was breakable and expensive. That was the point of our business. Per usual, not long after giving me a pep talk about buckling down and finishing the move, Jake was on a mission, delivering something important to someone elsewhere. Actually he said he had a list of deliveries to make. I was more than half convinced that it was no coincidence that as soon as physical labor was involved, he was out the door delivering items that weighed less than a pound but were, "Too precious to be mailed."

Yeah right. Two hours after he'd left, I'd spilled the contents of an antique oil lamp all over myself, so I'd taken a quick shower and was wearing my zip front, ratty purple chenille robe and favorite black UGGs. All covered with dust almost immediately. Jake had called and said he was going by the bank to see about a line of credit before he made his last delivery. He warned me he might not get back until after seven. I warned him that tomorrow he was dealing with the shop and I was getting my hair done.

Alone, I worked through lunch and most of the afternoon, sorting items and packing the smaller trinkets and vases. At four, I'd planned to stop, take another shower, get dressed in something decent, and start dinner, but I gotten distracted by a large chest of Civil War era uniforms, clothing, and memorabilia. The original velvet lining of the trunk was missing and someone had glued old newspapers and letters to the wood as a poor man's replacement. The trunk had been in the store since before Jake and I were married. He'd told me he'd purchased it and a houseful of furniture from an estate sale in Pennsylvania. One of his first big purchases when he opened the shop. Jake had admitted he'd had some rough years when he started dealing antiques full time. At one point he'd had to consider selling the house, but he'd managed to hold on until he built up his client list. We weren't rich by any means, and didn't have a lot saved for emergencies, but we were for the most part comfortable. The furnace purchase was a setback.

I didn't actually have to move every single item in the shop. But there had to be a clear path to the door. I'd lost count of how many trips I'd made up the stairs to the living room which had become antiques central when I heard the shop doorknob rattle. I paused on the step. Another rattle and someone shook the door, as if it were stuck, not locked. The shades were drawn. The sign in the window made it clear that we were closed. It was late afternoon, already dark outside, and I could see the large shadow of a person behind the shade.

"We're closed. Please come back next week." I shouted from the steps.

Again, someone twisted the doorknob. I put the crystal lamp that I was carrying down on the landing and descended.

I flipped on the entry light and peeked through the shade.

"Open up Ms. Cohen."

Richard Baez shook the doorknob again.

Reluctantly I unlocked the dead bolt and opened the door halfway. "Did your father send you? Are you dropping off tools for tomorrow?"

He shook his head and in any case, he was empty-handed. "I saw Mr. Cohen's Tahoe wasn't here."

"And?" I couldn't figure out what he wanted.

"You're such a little woman. Figure you could use some help moving stuff."

His smile was creepy, just this shade short of a leer. I pulled my robe tighter around me. I could smell beer and marijuana. He must have gotten off work early.

"Thanks, but I'm fine. I'll see you and your father tomorrow morning."

I started to close the door, but he stuck his foot in the doorway.

"Come on Valentine. That's such a cool name. Let me in. You can tell me the stories behind some of that old stuff you sell."

Since when did I stop being Mrs. Cohen? I kept up the pressure on the door.

"No thanks. I'm fine."

His face darkened. "Why won't you let me help you? You should treat me with more respect."

He gave a little push on the door and I stumbled backwards. I scrambled to regain my balance.

"Go home, Richard."

His face was beet red. "Don't be that way. I've seen how you look at me."

He walked closer.

I felt nauseous. "Leave right now or I'm calling your father."

"My father's on a job." He laughed. The beer and weed were definitely in charge. "What are you wearing under that robe? How about a peek?"

"Forget your father I'm calling the cops." Jake stood in the doorway of the shop, holding his phone.

Richard held up his hands. "Hey, I was just trying to help, Mr. Cohen. No harm, no foul."

"Get out. You're through here."

"What about my father? He'll kill me. You got to let us...."

"I don't have to let you do anything. You explain it to your father any way you can. But you're done. Walk in this shop again and I'll have you arrested for trespassing."

Richard blew past Jake, then whirled around. "You'll be sorry. I know about you. And your family. It's not just her. Everybody knows you're both crazy."

He stormed off and like Scarlet O'Hara, I collapsed in my husband's arms.

***

"I needed the directions to the Stewart house," Jake said, when I finally got around to asking him why he'd come back to the house early. "I wrote them down on the back of an envelope and forgot to take it with me."

I made a mental note not to ever complain about him not having GPS in his Tahoe. Or at least not to complain about it for a long, long time.

My two favorite detectives had arrived about two hours after Jake make the 9-1-1 call. Apparently crime was rampant in Seamont that afternoon and my confrontation with a plumber was only mildly interesting. A bored patrol officer had taken down the information and had me sign a statement, letting me know someone would go speak with Richard in the next day or two. He'd advised us to change our locks. I'd assumed that was the end of it, but the police computer must have my name flagged because Detectives Ellison and Hardesty showed up without me asking for them.

"Describe your relationship with Richard Baez." Detective Hardesty was poised to write down all the salacious details in his notebook.

I glanced at Jake and sighed. "What's next? Are you going to ask me what I was wearing? Why I opened the door to him, knowing I was alone?"

Detective Ellison intervened. "No. We just need to know if you were friends or business acquaintances. Was this confrontation personal or do you think it was related to your connection to the Berman or Chang murders. We need to know how much of a threat you think this Richard Baez is."

Jake started to answer her but I held up a hand stopping him. "I got this."

I pointed towards Detective Ellison. "Why should I speak to you, either of you? You've lied to me since the day you walked in our shop. Bad enough I can't trust the police to tell me the truth, now I'm absolutely certain that no matter what you say, you can't protect me. Someone sliced my tire in the police parking lot, for heaven's sake." My voice got louder with each word. "You know what? I'm done. No more trips to murder scenes, no more watching suspects be interviewed. I going to do what my husband wanted all along, concentrate on our lives, our business, and our family."

At some point during my tirade, Jake had wrapped an arm around my shoulders.

Detective Hardesty cleared his throat. "Sorry. We were–"

Detective Ellison took over again. "Hey, so we lied to you. Get over it. We needed to clear you as suspects in the Berman murders. We did that and you gave us some decent leads to follow up. I'm not here to make friends, I have to catch a murderer before he kills again."

Jake tried to answer. "What Val is trying to say–"

"I can talk for myself. You should have told us the truth. I fed you cinnamon rolls!"

Detective Ellison shrugged. "Not like they were homemade or anything!"

Jake's hold on me tightened, keeping me from moving forward. "This would be a good time for both of you to leave. It's late and Val's had a very bad day."

"Yeah, right." Detective Ellison wisely took a step back and gave me a sympathetic nod. "Sorry. But forget Baez for a minute and tell us about the tire? Sliced? Someone used a knife on it? When did that happen? Do you still have the tire?"

"You think the killer was the one who slashed my tire? I told Jake it wasn't kids." I shrugged off Jake's arm and headed towards the kitchen. "I have the name of the garage owner. He probably still has the tire."

"Great," Detective Ellison followed me. "Sorry about the crack about the cinnamon rolls, they were really good. Can you give me the name of the bakery too?"

"Sure. It's called *Betsy's Bread and More.* I think they use a special brown sugar."

"Really?"

"Yeah. Their yeast rolls are good. Almost as good as my mother-in-law's."

"And don't worry about Richard Baez. I'll make sure he's put back on a leash."

As I opened the kitchen door, I glanced back in time to see Jake and Detective Hardesty staring at each other in disbelief.

CHAPTER 11

"Are you okay?"

"No." I was sitting on the side of our bed in a cotton nightshirt contemplating the passion pink polish on my toenails and wondering how I could have been so blind to what Richard Baez had been thinking and planning. Some psychic I was.

Jake turned off the bathroom light and walked over, a damp towel slung around his hips. He sat down on the bed beside me.

"Can I get you something? Something to drink? Tea or...maybe some hot chocolate?"

"Hot chocolate?" An image flashed in my mind of his mother bringing him a cup of hot chocolate and explaining that his life wasn't over because he didn't make the cut for the basketball team. On the heels of that, another. A teenaged Jake was sitting at the kitchen table, the same one we have now, fixing himself a cup of hot chocolate. He was wearing a dark suit. There had been a death. A funeral. His grandfather I guessed.

"Stop it," Jake warned, a playful tone belying his words. "I know that expression. You're rifling through my memories, aren't you?"

"Not on purpose." I smiled at him and accepted his offer of comfort. "I'd love a cup of hot chocolate."

He stroked the long braid that was hanging over my right shoulder. "With marshmallows, I suppose?"

Instead of answering I turned sideways and wrapped my arms around him. My face buried in his chest, I let go. Sobbing, I confessed, "I was so scared today. I didn't have any warning. I should have known, should have had some inkling that Richard....I didn't see it, Jake. I'm so sorry, I didn't see it."

He held me, rubbing my back, telling me he loved me and reminding me that he understood better than anyone that despite my considerable talents, being all-knowing wasn't one of them.

I only cried harder. Not because his words weren't what I needed, but because his words made me feel safe enough to let down all my defenses. I cried for the Changs. For the Bermans. For the teenaged Jake losing his grandfather. For the little boy or girl with the cape that didn't exist yet.

He pulled me on his lap, cradling me like a child.

Sometime later, I'd exhausted myself. Every tear had been expelled from my body.

"Jake, will you do something for me?" My voice was a hoarse whisper against his neck.

"Anything," he said, his hand moving to cup my cheek. "What?"

"Cut down a tree."

"What?"

"The tree you can see from the nursery window. Cut it down or move it."

"Can it wait until tomorrow?" He asked, shifting us so we were laying down. "It's dark out there now."

I nodded, closing my eyes and letting sleep begin to wash over me. "Anytime in the next couple of years. Just don't forget."

***

We hadn't remembered to set the alarm clock. As a consequence it was almost nine before I opened my eyes.

Jake was sleeping on his stomach next to me, the morning sun streaming through the window creating a warm pool of light on our bed.

I resisted the urge to stroke my hand down his bare back, I didn't want to wake him. At this moment I was perfectly content to stay cocooned under the covers, the events of the last few days held at bay.

Jake and I had a wedding anniversary coming up in about six weeks. He liked making a big deal out of it and I had to admit I enjoyed his enthusiasm for marking the day. We hadn't made any plans yet. Last year we had combined the celebration with a buying trip to Pennsylvania. We had spent two weeks driving around Lancaster County picking up some lovely furniture pieces. The owners of the bed and breakfast we'd stayed in had sent us a brochure not long ago. It was a nice reminder of our time there.

I closed my eyes and let my mind drift back there.

"Jake, you need to get out of there now and get dressed. We're going to be late."

"Ten more minutes." He stretched out and let his body float. "Hey, we should get a Jacuzzi for our house! This is great."

I smiled. Our room came with a two person Jacuzzi and I think Jake had spent at least an hour in it each day. I glanced in the mirror and added another layer of mascara. My hair was done. All I lacked was changing from my robe to the "little black" dress and the seriously high heels that went with it. "What about dinner? We have reservations. Remember you promised me white tablecloths and candles tonight."

"We could stay here instead," he suggested. "You could hop back in and–"

"Forget it. We did that last night and I never got dinner." I walked over and sat on the tiled edge. I leaned over and gave him a quick kiss. "Get out of there before my favorite parts shrink and get all pruney."

"Pruney? I'll give you pruney! I have many excellent parts and none of them are shrunken or pruney!" He sat up in the water and reached for me. "Come here and examine the evidence yourself."

Anticipating his reaction, I'd moved faster. From the other side of the room, I offered my apologies and a promise to verify his claims later.

"Val, are you awake?" The memory vanished.

Jake rolled over and pulled me close.

"Hmmm, maybe." I brushed my lips over his. "I was thinking about our anniversary. I guess with the furnace situation and the costs, we won't be taking a trip this year."

"Sorry. Sometimes this house is more of a burden than an asset." He sighed. "Maybe we could go somewhere close, just for a weekend?"

"Or we can just stay here and work on that project I've been putting off."

"Really?" Jake grinned. "Are you sure?"

"Yes." And I was. Finally. When we'd first married I'd wanted nothing more than to create a world where there was just the two of us. I wanted, no I needed, time to focus on Jake and our marriage. Plus there was the business. Jake had grown up knowing what he wanted to do with his life. He had just gotten his antique business in the black and I wanted to learn how to help him make it a success. I traveled to auctions with him, asked a million questions, and studied. A baby wouldn't have allowed me to do all that. Or at least that's the excuse I'd used.

"We don't have to wait for our anniversary to get started, do we?"

"No."

"Good." Jake tugged on my nightshirt, pulling it off over my head.

CHAPTER 12

Our regular FedEx guy was on vacation. His replacement had brought the package to the front door, instead of the shop entrance. I signed for it and then struggled down the steps with the unwieldy box, finally plopping it on the store counter.

"When's Hank back?" I grumbled.

Jake didn't look up from his laptop. "Another week."

"I hope he's back before you get that shipment from Elleridge. Otherwise we'll open up a branch office in the living room."

"Did you give the FedEx guy the package for the Smythes? I promised delivery by...."

"I shipped it out yesterday, don't you remember?"

He waved me off. "Sorry, I've been distracted with...."

He didn't have to finish the sentence. It wasn't like Jake. He was the organized one of us, but the murders had wreaked havoc with my husband's orderly mind.

"I've got to get a new system," he muttered. "A better way to track what's come in and what's shipped out. The

Elleridge stuff has been trickling in piece by piece. I hate that. I want to deliver it all to the client in one trip instead of...." He paused and acquired a funny look on his face. "I need to know what's come in and what's...."

"What's late?" I offered.

"Yeah. What's late? What isn't here when it's supposed to be here?"

Jake walked over to the storage closet in the far corner of the shop. He was mumbling to himself. "I wonder if I kept them up here or if they're in the basement."

"What are you talking about?"

"I want to look at the inventory of items I sold to the Changs. I gave a list to the police right after the murders, but I don't remember all the items. I'm not sure how far back the files up here...."

"Aren't they in the cold and dead files in the attic? Warm and dead are in the basement. They're the ones we thought might have a slight chance to live to be useful another day."

Jake stepped out of the closet to glare at me. "Sometimes your sense of humor is too damn grotesque."

I was only mildly ashamed. If I sometimes didn't laugh at all the images and thoughts that were constantly running amok in my head, it would probably kill me...pun intended.

"Got it," came the triumphant whoop from the closet.

Jake emerged, dusty, but holding a manila file aloft.

"You really should have the files scanned onto a disk and get rid of all that paper. It's a fire hazard."

He waved me off. "I have a system."

I knew about his famous system, which only he understood, and which he had just complained about.

"Let's get some coffee."

We sat at the dining room table as he spread out the folder full of receipts, indicating where Jake had bought each item, authenticity documentation, as well as photocopies of the cancelled checks from the Changs when he made deliveries to them.

He sifted through the paperwork, smiling as he remembered each piece. "They were good clients. Knew what they wanted and were willing to pay for it. Very diverse tastes. They bought some of my Civil War era stock. An early 19th Century bedroom set for a guest room. Some antique weapons. Old battlefield lithographs."

"I thought they liked Asian pieces? What about the Chinese screen?"

"Eclectic tastes. Early American. Asian. They liked what they liked. Here's the info on that Chinese screen. And this is the list of items I gave to the police, but...."

He ran his finger down the page. Then thumbed through the receipts again. He pulled out three photos stapled to documentation papers.

Jake checked it, then nodded.

"I'd forgotten. These were items that I bought from the same dealer who sold me the screen. You know the one in New Hope who sold me most of the Calvin Weatherly estate. Mr. Weatherly was another man who had money to indulge in whatever caught his eye. No rhyme or reason to his possessions."

"Here's a rare antique Nanking clock, dating from the 1800s. I'd showed the Changs a photo of it. It was to go on their mantle. They loved it."

He pointed to the next photo. "This was also a nineteenth century artifact. A very ornate Qing Dynasty Canton Export Card Case."

Even from the photo I could see how intricately carved the piece was.

"And then, just like I said, the Changs really did have eclectic taste. This photo is of a jewelry box from Weatherly's estate sale. It's a collectible from the 1904 St. Louis World's Fair. The Changs met at Washington University. He proposed under the famous arch. Mrs. Chang had a collection of World's Fair memorabilia and her husband had me find this piece. It was going to be an anniversary present. Dealer promised to send all of the items with the screen, but the order got fouled up. It came in two weeks after the murders."

"So did you return the stuff that never made it to the Changs?"

Jake shook his head. "No returns policy. I sold the clock and the card case, but...."

"But what?"

"You know I like World's Fair stuff so...."

I looked at him. "You kept the jewelry box?"

He nodded sheepishly.

"And who bought the other pieces?"

"Margo. She was decorating a home in Scarsdale. I didn't make as much as I'd hoped, but was just relieved to be able to sell them at all."

***

"I could kill him."

I was holding the fort down at the shop again while Jake made a delivery up in Katonah. Margo Cager, designer to Wall Street big boys, stood with her hands on her svelte hips in front of me. Margo had a love-hate relationship with my husband. She respected his expertise in antiquities and knew he was honest. But it drove her cr-cr-cr-crazy when he proved her wrong.

I smiled. "What now?"

"I found a vintage radio with bakelite knobs. Looked perfect and was significantly cheaper than what Jake said I had to pay. Told him I'd take care of it."

I nodded.

"I've been in this business for 10 years. I'm no amateur."

I gave her a weak smile. I was pretty sure, without the need for any premonitions, for how this story was going to turn out.

"I picked up the radio yesterday and took it up to that Bed and Breakfast I've been decorating."

"And?"

"The owners went ballistic. They're apparently bakelite fiends. Knew immediately that the knobs were fake. 'Mold marks,' they kept screaming. 'Didn't I know that bakelite was carved, not pressed in molds?' And they kept sniffing the radio. Said it didn't have a hint of Formaldehyde. The seller had given me documentation, but the owners said it was fake. Damn it, that's what I pay Jake to determine."

I murmured appropriate words of sympathy.

Margo helped herself to a handful of M&Ms that I keep on the counter. Then glanced around the shop.

"I don't suppose you have a 1940s radio with bakelite knobs? I promised to get another one and give it as a gift."

I shrugged. "Sorry. We don't have one here, but I know that Jake has a source for them in the city."

Jake might have been willing to eat into his profit when he lost the bidding war with Newton548, but since

Margo had screwed this up, no reason for us to pay the difference.

I added, "It's going to cost more. But you'll have proper documentation that you can show the clients. It will pass muster smell-wise, even the Formula 409 test."

Margo sighed and scooped up another handful of candies. "Yeah. I remember now. Jake went on and on about how to know the real from the fake. Honest to God, Val, sometimes your husband goes on a tear and I just smile and tune him out."

"Me too." We both giggled like schoolgirls.

"But I swear if your husband whispers any hint of 'I told you so'...."

I waved it off.

Margo took a final handful of candy. "Tell Jake I need it as soon as possible. I apologized enough for three lifetimes with the owners, but I want to be sure that they know I'm a pro. They've already bought another B&B in Litchfield and I want that job as well. This radio is an investment. If I get the Litchfield gig, they'll be plenty of commissions for the two of you and me."

Margo turned to leave, then stopped. "You got my new business cards?"

We kept a variety of decorators' cards on hand. Some buyers wanted more help decorating than Jake and I could give. I flipped through the pile and held up one of Margo's.

She shook her head. "No, that's my old one."

She took a handful of heavily embossed cards from her purse. "Use these instead. Had them made with my web site info."

"I thought you didn't think you needed a web site?"

Margo shrugged. "Got to keep moving forward or you get left behind. Pull it up on your screen, www.margocagerdesign.com."

The home screen showed a very large, quietly tasteful room. I recognized in the photo several antiques that we'd gotten for Margo. There were links to photos of other design projects that Margo had done and I spotted more of our commissions.

I was impressed. "Looks gorgeous, classy."

Margo grinned. "You mean expensive. I make no bones about it. I'm looking to attract a certain clientele."

She moved toward the door. "Tell that husband of yours that I need the radio pronto."

I wish I could say that some dark cloud suddenly darkened the entryway as Margo went through it, but it didn't. Sunny, gorgeous day through and through.

***

I made a clean getaway.

Jake had walked in the door from the city with the 1940s radio that Margo had ordered. Within three minutes, who should show up but his Mama.

I gave them both my most sincere smile, which nobody, least of all my mother-in-law, believed, and announced, "Why don't the two of you have a nice visit. I'll just run this over to Margo. She said it was urgent that she get it." With a nod to my husband, I added, "I'll also ask her if she still has any of those items that were originally purchased for the Changs."

It was really a win-win. My mother-in-law got her baby boy's undivided attention and I didn't have to listen to her make snide comments about me. I didn't even bother to call ahead to Margo's. This wasn't the first time we'd had to drop off merchandise. Margo had given me the passcode to the garage keypad. Worst case scenario, I'd leave the well-wrapped package on a counter in her three-car garage and go kill an hour or two at the mall. Best case, Margo and I would shoot the breeze until it was safe to return home.

I drove my bug up Weaver Street, past Five Corners, and down Popham Road. This was Scarsdale. The village of 17,000 ranked number one in America's top-earning towns. Average income was $300,000. If you looked hard, you could find some three bedroom ranch houses for a million plus, but it was more likely that you would trip over a dozen mega-mansions on any given block. Margo had decorated more than her fair share of them.

Her own little home sweet home was a 4,000 square foot brick colonial, set back from the street on an acre of land. In New York suburban terms, that was the equivalent of the Ponderosa spread. Most McMansions were situated on postage-stamped lots. But Margo was a very successful decorator and Mort Cager, her ex-husband, was an even more successful Wall Street mover and shaker. The breakup, four years earlier, had been nasty and brutish.

They even fought over custody of Heidi, a Greyhound that always looked underfed.

"Let's just say I know where Mort's buried the bodies," a slightly drunk Margo had confided over martinis one evening. "I know secrets that would make your skin crawl and your mother turn over in her grave."

"My mother's still alive, thank you very much." Of course, I'd seen more bodies spinning in their graves, figuratively speaking, than I cared to count or confide to Margo, even if I'd had a couple of martinis myself. "Everybody's got secrets, Margo."

God knows I had more than my fair share. I'd grown up in a household of women, my mother, my two aunts, my grandmother. All with varying degrees of "special intuition." I'd never known my father. He'd died before I was born in a car accident with my grandfather. They had driven across a bridge that was there one minute and gone the next. The story goes my grandmother had warned him for years to stay away from bridges, but he hadn't listened. Thinking about it, staying away from bridges would be almost impossible. I hoped I never had that kind of open-ended premonition about someone I loved. Some secrets should stay secrets, especially those about the future.

"Honey, I'll bet my secrets against yours any day. You are such an innocent. You are a good person, Val. A good friend." Margo had drunk enough that she was barely able to navigate the room to fix another martini. I was glad, I was slowly drowning a nearby fichus with the multiple drinks she'd continued to serve me despite my protests. I wondered how long it was going to take for the olives I'd buried in the potting soil to decompose.

"Val, I don't know that I believe in all that psychic stuff, but I know you mean well. You stay that way, stay sweet, don't look too hard at people, they'll disappoint you every time."

So Margo had emerged from her marriage with lots of money, lots of connections, the house, a slight alcohol problem, and shared custody of the dog.

I pulled into the circular driveway. Lights were on in the living room and in an upstairs bedroom. Motion-sensor lights on the front porch came on automatically as I got out of my car. I carried the bubble-wrapped radio up to the door and rang the bell. I could hear it echoing throughout the house. When no one came to the door, I used my cell phone to call, but both her home phone and her cell phone went straight to voice mail.

The three-car garage was on the side of the house, under what I knew to be the master bedroom suite. There was a spotlight over the first bay. I keyed in the code and the door went up slowly.

Margo's car was in the garage, but that didn't give me any pause. I didn't even hesitate when I saw the door to the basement was open. I just figured that Margo had come in and forgotten to close it. Maybe she'd had to rush in with groceries that needed refrigeration. More likely she needed to go to the bathroom. Or maybe the telephone was ringing off the hook.

What hadn't crossed my mind is that she'd never had a chance to close the door. That when she'd come into her lovely, gorgeous, expensive home, someone had been waiting for her.

Maybe my psychic radar was on the blink.

Red wasn't ever Margo's color, even in death. But red, blood red, was splashed everywhere. It clashed with the muted pumpkin and slate décor. But I guess the killer didn't know Margo's color palate. He only wanted her dead. I didn't check for a pulse. I didn't need to be a psychic to know that the killer knew how to wield a knife with speed, precision, and deadly aim.

I dropped the radio and ran, faster than I thought possible to my car. I don't think I took a breath until I was in the middle of the town's shopping district. I pulled over, under a street lamp, and hit speed dial one. It rang once, twice, and when Jake picked up, the words tumbled out fast and loud. "She's dead. Margo's dead. He struck again."

There was a pause. I'm sure it was hard to comprehend, even if the words were simple and direct. But I could hear the panic in his voice when Jake asked, "Where are you?"

I couldn't answer. I was going to be sick.

I dropped my cell phone on the passenger seat and opened the driver's door. I lost my dinner, maybe lunch, maybe even breakfast. I couldn't catch my breath.

I could hear Jake's screaming into the phone. "Where are you Val? Tell me where you are?"

Between dry heaves, I told him where I was.

"Lock the doors. I'll be there in ten minutes."

I slid back into the car and hit the automatic locks. It didn't matter anymore. I'd failed and another person was dead. This time it was someone who'd claimed me as a friend.

CHAPTER 13

Once Jake had gotten me calmed down, he'd called the police and given them Margo's address and our contact info. They ordered us to meet the police at the house. We took his Tahoe. My car smelled of vomit.

The Medical Examiner pulled up about fifteen minutes after the Scarsdale police had come roaring up the street, sirens screaming and flashing lights ablaze. Once the information had been broadcast over the police scanner, it wasn't long before television crews had set up base camp at the end of the driveway. This was big news: Wealthy enclave, horrific crime despite the elaborate security systems that all these mini-mansions had. It was the stuff of Lifetime movies. In fact, I was pretty sure that some writer was working on the plot before Margo's body had even been brought out of her house.

Despite the cold, dark hour, neighbors were clustered together, trying to make sense of what had happened–and figure out how it wasn't going to happen to them. Jake and

I had been ordered to stay in our car until a detective could talk to us.

"Think we'll get a ticket for overnight parking?"

I didn't recognize my voice. It was gravelly, like a rock singer at the end of a two-hour concert, screaming lyrics at overwrought teenyboppers. Except I'd just been screaming, no lyrics involved.

"Don't worry about it." Jake's voice sounded perfectly normal.

"I'll fight any ticket. I'll go to night court and just explain...."

Jake shot me a look. "Explain what, exactly?"

"That I'd just discovered...and I was scared...so I...."

My argument before the court sounded better in my head than when I said it out loud.

Jake gave one of his patient smiles. The 'I'll humor the poor crazy woman I've married' look.

"I guess maybe the parking ticket is the least of my worries."

Jake tapped the tip of my nose. "Bingo."

"The cops might think I had something to do with Margo's murder."

Jake nodded, encouraging me to continue down the path that now seemed obvious.

"I've discovered one too many dead bodies."

Jake smiled. "You're a regular Jessica Fletcher, tripping over murders every time you walk out of your house."

I giggled and then laughed until tears ran down my face. Of course, that was the moment that a detective knocked on my window. Undoubtedly, he'd report that the woman who'd barged obliviously into a murder scene found it all very funny. Heck, might as well throw the switch on the electric chair right then.

Detective Mark Santoni slid into the backseat. He and his partner had been the first ones on the scene. He took out a small tape recorder. "This makes it easier than trying to write down exactly what you tell me. Okay?"

Of course we nodded yes, although I'd never seen a cop with a tape recorder in all those years of watching *Law and Order*. Would my words come back to trip me up?

"Why don't you tell me what happened, Mrs. Cohen?"

Seemed a simple enough task. I explained that I was dropping off an antique radio that no one had answered the door, so I was going to leave it in the garage.

Santoni nodded. "You knew the security code?'

"Yes. Margo, the woman who...." I couldn't bring myself to say the *dead woman.* "Anyway, Margo had given me the code years ago. I've dropped off items before when she wasn't home."

"Was the cover to the keypad up or down?"

I had to think. "Up, it was definitely up. Why is that important?"

Santoni shrugged. "Maybe a fingerprint on the cover."

I tried to be careful and concise about what had happened, but once I'd crossed the threshold into Margo's basement and saw the bloody scene, it all became a blur, just flashes of red oozing from the gaping holes in Margo's body, smeared on the walls and floor.

I started to get sick again. I opened the door to get some air.

Jake rubbed my back. "Can we do this tomorrow? I'd like to take my wife home."

Santoni's voice was firm. "No." His tone softened. "The first hours after a crime are critical."

I settled back in my seat and turned to face him. "I really don't remember much else. It was such a nightmare. I dropped the radio and ran."

"Where?"

"To Scarsdale village. I left my car in a no-parking zone. Maybe you could tell the parking...."

Santoni shook his head. "Where did you drop the radio?"

"On the floor."

"Where on the floor?" Santoni's voice sounded like he was talking to a very young child.

I thought for a moment. "I dropped it maybe two feet into the room, near...near the body."

Santoni held up a hand. "Wait here a minute."

He got out of the car and motioned to his partner. They chatted a few moments, then walked back into the garage.

"What's it all about? You think I messed up the crime scene by dropping the radio?"

Jake shrugged.

Santoni came back and motioned for Jake to put down the passenger side window. "You're sure you didn't take the radio with you. Maybe you left it in your car in the village?"

I was confused, but not that confused. "No. I dropped it in the basement. Why?"

Santoni frowned. "Because it's not there now."

Jake gasped.

I still didn't understand. It was like my mind couldn't compute what Jake and the detective clearly understood. "What does that mean?

Jake grabbed my hand. "Val, it means that the killer was still in the house when you found Margo."

***

I didn't think I'd ever sleep. The images of blood-splattered walls, the Changs, the Bermans, and now Margo, were seared into my brain. And yet, when we finally got home around three in the morning, I fell into bed, fully clothed, and slept the sleep of the dead, no pun intended.

I couldn't tell if the pounding I heard was a dream, a premonition, or simply someone using a fist on our front door.

"Who the hell is that?" Jake mumbled before pulling a pillow over his head.

A quick glance at the clock indicated it was barely 6 AM.

Any hope that ignoring the pounding would make it go away quickly evaporated, as it got louder and more persistent. I dragged myself down to the front door and flipped on the porch light. Once I saw who it was, I turned to go back to bed.

"Open up Val."

Diane Ellison raised the brass knocker to reinforce her order.

I didn't have any fight left in me. I opened the front door, but when Diane started to speak, I held up my hand to staunch the flow of questions or lectures. I motioned her to follow me to the kitchen. I wasn't about to do another ten rounds with a cop without some coffee. I rooted around in the bread box for a bagel, but had to settle for a bag of Oreos. Chocolate and caffeine were needed.

The kitchen table was covered with antiques, relocated from the shop while we were awaiting oil tank repairs. I poured two mugs, grabbed mine and the cookies, and headed for the living room. I wasn't going to be the hostess with the mostest at that hour. Diane could help herself.

Sitting in the living room wasn't much easier. Navigating a path through vintage tables, stacks of china, and artwork was almost more than my sleep-deprived brain could accomplish. I finally reached the sofa and sank down into the soft cushions. It was still dark outside so I reached up and turned on the nearest lamp. Diane perched on a nearby Windsor chair.

"I should have been your first call."

She sounded more peeved than official.

I shrugged. "Jake was in charge of contacting the cops. I was trying to remember how to breathe."

I took a sip of coffee and nibbled on a cookie.

"Now that a few hours have passed, do you remember seeing or hearing anything? You know they assume that the killer was still there when you found Ms. Cager. Try Val. Walk it through, but try to remember sounds, shadows."

The last thing I wanted to do was relive the previous 10 hours. This wasn't like the movie where the story replayed over and over until the ending was a happy one. No matter what I remembered, Margo would still be dead. I'd miss her.

I was saved by more knocking at the front door.

Diane frowned. "You expecting someone?"

"You think killers knock at the door?" With a grunt, I heaved myself off the sofa and headed for the front door. More surprises. I pushed my hair back and wondered if I should get dressed. It seemed like my day had officially started.

Instead I opened the door. "What are you doing here?"

It was Zeke Harrison.

"Sorry to bother you Ms. Cohen, but I was already on the road for a pickup at Clark Galleries when I heard the news. I passed your house, saw the police car, and just thought I'd check on you and Mr. Cohen."

How kind. Diane wanted information, gruesome details; Zeke was just checking on someone he knew.

I sighed. "We're okay. Well as okay as we can be under the circumstances."

"Zeke?"

Jake had given up sleeping.

"Like I said. Sorry to bother you, Mr. Cohen, but I was on my way to Clark's, saw the cop car, and...."

Jake rubbed the back of his neck. "As long as you're going there, would you mind taking a few boxes for the Monday auction? I planned to run them over today, but...."

He didn't have to finish his thought.

Zeke stepped in. "Where are they?"

Jake looked at me for help.

"I think most of the items are in the living room, but they're not boxed yet."

Zeke smiled. He pointed to Jake. "You get the packing material and I'll…"

Jake headed to the basement, and Zeke followed me into the living room. I could tell Diane wasn't happy to have company for her interrogation. But at least so far, I wasn't under arrest.

"Detective Ellison, this is Zeke Harrison. He runs his own company, moving antiques throughout the tri-state area."

"Did you know Margo Cager?"

So much for the pleasantries.

Zeke nodded. "Yes ma'am. A little. I've taken some items from here over to her house."

Diane sat up a little straighter. "When was the last time you were there?"

Zeke checked with me. "Maybe six months ago? That English settee you found for her."

I nodded. "Most times, Jake or I deliver to Margo. The items are usually decorative, but that settee was too big for Jake's Tahoe."

Zeke cleared his throat. "I think Ms. Cager uses Mazin Trucking for most of her deliveries."

Again, I nodded. "You're right. She's been using Ralph Mazin for years."

Diane made a note on her pad. "When you went there, did you go in through the garage?"

"Ms. Cager met me in the driveway. She opened the garage door, then the basement door. We carried it in to her office space."

"We?"

Zeke looked nervous. "Yes, ma'am. Couldn't carry it by myself. Jeff Smith was working with me that day."

Diane paused. "Can you give me his contact information?"

Zeke shook his head. "No ma'am. Haven't seen or heard from him in a few months."

"No forwarding address? Where did you send his paycheck? Can you describe him?"

Zeke looked miserable. Luckily, Jake walked back into the living room carrying empty boxes and packing material. He looked around the group and caught my raised eyebrow. He launched into his hale fellow routine.

"Zeke, can you grab that table lamp and spittoon. We'll go back in the kitchen where some of the other stuff is."

Zeke moved with lightning speed, but not before Diane added, "If you hear from Jeff, call me."

Zeke nodded and was gone.

I blew out a breath. Diane was being deliberately dense. "Come on. Zeke doesn't hand out 1099s to the Jeff Smiths of this world. You know Smith's probably not even his real name. Zeke picked him up at Calvary Park for help that day."

Calvary Park was a corner in Mamaroneck where laborers, most of them undocumented immigrants, waited.

Landscapers, contractors, truckers, even homeowners who had small projects, could always find someone to do grunt work for 50 bucks cash at the end of the day.

Diane finished the last of her coffee. "Probably, but I'm going to ask around. Let's meet at headquarters later today. Maybe you'll have a better memory of last night."

"I don't want to remember what I saw."

Zeke came into the room and picked up a wooden stool and some china figurines.

Diane put on her coat. "You better hope you remember something. The killer knows you were there. He took the package you brought Mrs. Cager. We don't know any more than we did when the Bermans were killed. Somebody is on a killing spree and we don't know why."

"I don't know anything. If I did, I'd tell you."

Zeke reached past me. "Excuse me. Don't mean to interrupt."

I moved and he grabbed a pair of brass candlesticks.

Diane stopped at the front door. "Meet me at two at headquarters."

It didn't sound like a request.

CHAPTER 14

I settled back on the couch while Jake and Zeke went downstairs to pick up a few more items for Clark's auction. I must have dozed off because when I woke up, I was covered in an afghan my mother had crocheted for my first apartment.

"You're awake." Jake stood in the hall, a mug in one hand, the *New York Times* in the other.

My mouth felt fuzzy. I'd slept, but still felt sluggish.

"Zeke gave me the name of Hank Fenwick, a cousin of his who's a plumber. The guy will be by later today. In the meantime, Zeke's moving things around. I just came up to get some coffee."

"Any mention of...." I nodded toward the newspaper.

He joined me on the sofa. "Nope. The story is online, but too late for the early print edition. I checked the web editions of the *New York Post* and *Daily News*. They're all over the story like gum on a shoe."

I sniffed. "Tabloid heaven."

Jake nodded. "Sure. Rich designer, wealthy suburb, and Mort Cager has been under investigation by the Securities and Exchange Commission for a couple of months. Papers are suggesting there's a connection between Margo's death and the Feds case of Mort's insider trading"

"Alleged insider trading," I warned.

"Trust me. It's not alleged, it's real. Margo hinted she had the goods on her ex-. Her decorating business was just beginning to recover from the economic meltdown. Wall Street bonuses, the lifeblood of her business."

"And ours." I remembered some very tight months.

"Yep, and ours. But Margo was still living large even in the midst of what I know were tough times for decorators. Mort Cager's generous alimony was making up the difference."

"What about Heidi? No one found her at the house last night. Does Mort have her?" I hated the thought of the dog wandering the streets or the killer taking her.

"Reporters caught Mort at a hotel in Boston this morning. He declined to give an interview but the dog was in the photo."

Suddenly I felt a lot better. "Good. So Margo's death is just a case of a divorce gone bad? You play with fire, you're going to get burned."

Feeling hungry, I jumped up. "Come on, I'll make some pancakes and bacon, but don't tell your mother."

Jake pulled me back down next to him. "Val."

His voice was quiet, serious.

"What?"

"It might be Mort, but...."

I didn't want to hear it. "I'm not suggesting that Mort did it himself. He probably hired a hit man."

"You don't think it's too much of a coincidence that Margo was killed the same way the Bermans and Changs, were slaughtered? That the killer used a knife to force Newton548 to swallow those pills?"

I was swimming frantically towards the only life preserver I had. "Maybe...maybe Margo's killer was trying to make it look like...You know, maybe he was a copycat killer."

Jake shrugged. "Maybe."

He didn't sound convinced.

My appetite vanished.

I snuggled up against Jake, who held me close. The steady thrum of his heartbeat was comforting. I fought against the endless loop of blood-splattered images that threatened to drown me.

Jake's voice startled me. "You know what I can't figure."

"Besides the identity of the psycho killer running rampant?"

Jake chuckled. "Well, there's that."

His voice got serious again. "But I can't see why anyone would kill for a radio with bakelite knobs. It cost $150. Even if she marked it up 100 percent, it doesn't seem worth murder."

I sat up. "I think that the radio was just a bonus. I mean, Margo didn't even know I was coming over to deliver it, so the killer...."

"Didn't know either," Jake finished. "So why take it? Why grab the radio?"

"Mr. Cohen?"

Zeke was standing in the hallway holding a box marked Chinese pendants.

Jake stood. "I'm sorry. I meant to come right back down and help you."

Zeke waved him off. "Moved things around. Put a couple of the more breakable pieces in that storage closet with your files. Wondered if I could combine some of the smaller Chinese statues with this box?"

Jake shook his head. "No. I'm heading into the city later today. Taking them to a jeweler down in the Village. I'll finish up downstairs so it's ready when the plumber comes."

Jake reached for his wallet. He took out two twenty dollar bills.

"No sir," Zeke insisted. "I just wanted to be sure you and Mrs. Cohen were okay. I have to be going. I'll stop by later today, make sure Hank is doing a good job."

With Zeke gone and Jake down in the shop, I was left with just my thoughts, none of which were good. I had an hour before I had to meet Diane. I needed coffee if I had any hope of being coherent. But first a shower, although I was sure that I'd never be able to scrub the image of Margo sprawled on the floor, dead eyes staring at me...or maybe her killer...from my mind.

***

I was on time for my meeting with Diane but she wasn't. She and her partner, Detective Hardesty, had been sent out on a new case. Another murder. This one in their jurisdiction and according to the desk sergeant, it involved illegal drugs and rival suppliers. Apparently Diane had forgotten about our appointment or maybe Chief Peterson thought stopping a possible gang war took precedence over a serial killer. Either way I didn't have to spend the afternoon in the police station being interrogated so I wasn't too upset at being stood up.

Since I was already out and Jake seemed to have the shop and the plumbers under control, I decided to pop over to the mall and do a little retail therapy. I needed a new pair of black slacks and Jake could use some new shirts.

"Hi, Honey."

"Interview over?"

I could hear some banging in the background. I hoped the new plumbers weren't having to take out a wall.

"Diane had to go investigate a fresher murder. I'm at the mall. That men's store you like has dress shirts on sale. You want me to pick you up a couple? The cuffs on your favorite gray shirt are looking ragged. You mother pointed that out to me last week."

"My shirt is fine. Listen, have you seen the box of vintage comic books that I picked up from Skeeters, the store in New Rochelle that was going out of business?"

I thought for a moment and drew a blank. "Nope."

"You didn't move it upstairs when we were clearing a path for the plumbers? Red cardboard box, about half-filled. There were some expensive first editions in it."

"I know what you're talking about, I just don't remember seeing it. Maybe it's in the storage room."

Jake sighed. "I didn't see it."

"Look again. There's so much stuff in there, you might have missed it. Also check behind the couch in the living room, and maybe under the kitchen table."

"Okay, I'll look around some more. I can't wait until we can get back to normal around here. You're not going to spend all afternoon shopping are you?"

"No." Not that I hadn't thought about it. Wandering around the mall had taken my mind off Margo and the Bermans for a little while. I hadn't found the black slacks I wanted but had picked up a few other things. "I'm about done unless you need something from here?"

"Nothing from the mall but we're out of milk and bread. Have you thought about dinner? I'm starving."

I looked down at the half-eaten hot pretzel in front of me and felt a little guilty. I'd only planned to get a cup of coffee but the odors of the food court had been too much temptation. I'd have to think of a better excuse for the two pairs of shoes and the dress in the bags next to me.

"I'll stop by the grocery store. See you in about an hour, okay?"

"Fine. Just be home before dark. There's still a person out there who–"

I could hear someone calling for "Mr. Cohen."

"Val, I have to go. Drive safely."

***

I was coming out of the grocery store when I got the feeling that I was being watched. My shopping cart was loaded down. We'd been eating too much takeout lately and it was past time I planned a few meals.

The parking lot had been filled when I'd arrived so I'd had to park in the far corner. When I pulled in, the spots around me had been taken, but now, it was just me and a black pickup that I recognized. Baez Plumbing.

I considered going back to the store, but I had milk and ice cream in my bags. I needed to get home. Besides it was still light outside and I was tired, so very tired of being afraid of bogeymen, the ones I knew and the ones who were still lurking.

Richard was leaning against the back of my car, arms folded. His face was beet red and I could smell the combination of weed and alcohol five feet away.

"You sicced the cops on me. I didn't do nothing." He stood up, looming over my grocery cart, his words slurred.

"Get out of my way or I'm calling the police." I reached for my purse, but he snatched it out of the cart and dangled it over my head.

"You've got to listen to me." He took a step forward.

I glanced around but there was no one in the immediate area.

"My father kicked me out of the house. Told me I was an embarrassment to the family. If you give him the job, maybe he'll take me back."

I reached for my purse, but he moved it out of reach. I tried to keep my voice low, calm, unthreatening. "I'm sorry. We've already hired another company."

"No. No way. Baez Plumbing does the work in your house. You can't just hire some other bastards. Who are they?"

I hated that my voice was wavering. "It doesn't matter. It's done. They're finishing the job right now."

"You bitch. It's all your fault."

He hurled my purse across the parking lot, then tossed my grocery cart on its side. The eggs spilled out of the bag, oozing yellow yolks spreading across the macadam.

I could see the veins in his neck pulsating. He took another step towards me, hands balled into fists.

"Help." I screamed as loud as I could.

An elderly man parked two rows away yelled, "You get away from her, you thug. I got the cops on their way."

The old man started to weave his way around parked cars to get to me. Richard glanced from me to the old man, then wheeled around and yanked open his truck door.

"This isn't over, bitch."

As he peeled out of the parking lot, tires squealing, the tarp over the truck bed blew off. It was only a few seconds before the truck was out of sight, but I was pretty sure that amidst the tool boxes and empty beer bottles, I'd caught a glimpse of a bright red cardboard box.

CHAPTER 15

I should have waited until after dinner to tell Jake about my latest encounter with Richard Baez. That was my plan. Instead when he remarked on the poor job the packer at the grocery had done and held up a cracked pickle jar, I explained that Richard really wanted us to rehire his father and hadn't liked my answer. I didn't have to be a psychic to know how Jake was going to react. He went ballistic. Shouting first at me for getting myself in that situation in the first place and then again on the telephone at Detective Ellison who was still up to her eyeballs in drug dealers and not in the best of moods to endure being chewed out by my husband. I gave her the short version of the evening's events, then passed the phone back to Jake, who had thought of a dozen other issues he had with the way the police were handling the threats to my safety and the investigation into the Bermans' murders.

I swallowed a couple of aspirin in anticipation of a looming headache and put away the rest of the groceries by myself, reflecting on Richard's craziness. Again the man had blindsided me. I'd been lucky to have gotten away with just a few broken eggs and a cracked jar of pickles.

Mr. Landon, the older gentleman who had confronted Richard, had assisted me afterward in righting my shopping cart and gathering up my groceries. He had also insisted on notifying the store manager about the hooligans lying in wait in the parking lot accosting innocent shoppers.

The manager had apologized profusely, replaced my damaged items, and I suspect more to shut up Mr. Landon than to compensate me, given us each a half dozen steaks and a bottle of wine to sooth the trauma. He'd offered to call the police, but I'd declined.

Damn, I hadn't noticed the pickles. To my credit, I was only delaying giving Jake the news, hoping we could have a nice, quiet dinner by ourselves without the presence of police.

Sighing, I put the steaks in the freezer, made Jake a sandwich for when he stopped ranting, and took the bottle of wine upstairs. I wanted a long soak in the old claw-footed bathtub in the bathroom attached to our bedroom.

"Long" turned out to be about 30 minutes and only because I locked the bathroom door.

"Val?" Jake rattled the doorknob. "Why is this door locked? Detective Ellison will be here first thing in the morning to take your statement."

"Oh, goody. Now go away. I left your dinner on the counter next to the microwave."

"Is that sarcasm?"

"No, it's leftover roast beef on rye."

"Funny. Why do you have the door locked, Val?"

"So I could be alone. I needed some alone time. I also needed a bubble bath."

"Why do you sound like you've been drinking?"

"Because I have. A very mediocre merlot. It was a gift from Phil."

"Phil? Who's Phil?"

"Phil the guy at the grocery store. Nice man. He knew your father. No wait. That was Mr. Landon. I don't know his first name. Mr. Landon knew your father. He couldn't remember if he'd met your mother or not. I assured him that he would have remembered if he had."

"Do I need to go find the spare key to this door or can you get out of the tub by yourself?"

"I'm not drunk, just buzzed. It wasn't that big a bottle."

"You drank the whole bottle? Valentine, don't move and don't fall asleep. I'll find the key."

"It's in the trinket box on my vanity table...your mother's vanity table. Promise me that I can pick the furniture for the baby's room. I want some stuff in this house that's just ours, not your family's."

"I can't find the key. Where did you see it last?"

"I saw it in the back of Richard's truck."

"What? I'm talking about the bathroom key. What are you talking about?"

"Your comics. The red box. I think Richard stole them. And you thought he just wanted me. Fooled you. Fooled me too."

"Damn it, Val. What else haven't you told me?"

"Your beard. I lied to you last year. I never liked your beard."

"Keeping talking. I'm getting a screwdriver and a hammer to take the door off the hinges."

***

"Good morning, Sunshine."

I made an appropriate noise in response as I walked past my too cheerful husband on my way to the coffee pot. My head was pounding and my stomach was queasy.

"My mother looked in on you earlier. She saw the new plumber and I had to explain why Javier wasn't working for us anymore. She did know your Mr. Landon. His first name is Saul by the way."

"That's nice," I mumbled, filling a mug with the dark brew. Great. His mother saw me sleeping off a hangover. I'm sure I just added another big black mark in the book Ruth Cohen was writing about her unsuitable daughter-in-law. "Did she say anything else?"

Jake continued typing into his laptop. "Nothing worth mentioning. Didn't say anything about you snoring or drooling on her pillow case. Oh, wait. She said she liked your new dress but that pink really isn't your color."

"It's not pink. It's blush. Wait. She opened my shopping bags?"

"Tiny little bit. Just took a peek."

"Jake!"

"Come on, you know she loves clothes."

"She needs to go visit some of your other relatives. Do a little traveling, if you know what I mean."

"Hell!"

"Well, maybe not there."

"Not my mother. Newton548. He's on-line again."

"That's quite a trick. He's dead." I walked over and starred at the eBay page view of an autographed Mickey Mantle baseball card. "He's also winning."

Jake clicked a few keys, raising the bid a few dollars. "Someone must have hacked his account."

"When?" I suddenly wondered if all of the bids that Newton548 had placed in the past were really his. For that matter, was he really dead? Was the man we found in the house on Newton Street really Newton548?

***

"You don't look so good, Val," Detective Ellison commented as I showed her into the living room about an hour later.

"It's been a tough week, Diane." We both sat down on the sofa, and I poured her tea using Ruth Cohen's best china set. I was in the mood for some civility and calm. "Have you arrested Richard Baez yet?"

"No. There's an APB out on him. His father thinks he might have left the country."

"Left the country?"

"Canada."

"I see."

Noting my displeasure, she added, "If he comes back, I'll arrest him. Handcuffs and everything."

"No extradition, Diane?" I was only half joking. I dreaded the next time Richard Baez jumped out of the shadows at me. I was convinced there would be a next time. Maybe I should starting carrying pepper spray or as Jake had suggested on more than one occasion, get a dog. A big, mean-looking dog, not one of those cute purse puppies.

"No extradition for cracked eggs, Val."

"Broken pickle jar too. Jake has discovered that some collectable comics are missing. Serious money involved now."

"Ah. Well...I'll see how to go about putting in a request to the State Department." Detective Ellison sighed. "Let's put a pin in the Richard Baez situation for the moment and talk about your friend Margo Cager and her ex-husband."

"Friend? Margo was a client." I paused to rethink that statement. "No, you're right. She was a friend too." I took a sip of tea. "Are you handling that murder now?"

"Only if I can prove a connection to the Bermans and the Changs' murders. Have you noted the body count lately? A lot of dead people cross your path, Val."

My stomach clenched. The detective had no idea. Putting down my tea cup, I looked her in the eyes. "Diane, I have never killed anything or anyone in my life."

She nodded. "I believe you. But I also believe you have a connection to the Changs and the Bermans' killer. Before you ask, yes, I think the same person who killed the Changs, killed the Bermans. Chief Peterson isn't convinced, but I am. Margo Cager's death may or may not be related to the other murders. Right now her husband is looking good for that."

"What about Newton548?"

"The old man? Stan Freedman's cause of death is listed as heart attack brought on by over-medication. I think I can scratch him off my homicide list. Unless of course there is something new you want to share with me?"

I still didn't know a way to convince her that Stan Freedman's death was murder. At least not yet. Now that Newton548 was back on-line, perhaps Jake and I could find him. I had a strong suspicion that instead of me being the link to all the murders, it was the person posing as Newton548.

***

While Detective Ellison took a call from her partner, and with my hangover ebbing and hunger pangs catching my attention, I went to the kitchen for some cookies to add to the tea tray. The cookies weren't homemade, but they were from the bakery where I'd gotten the cinnamon rolls, my friend Diane loved so much. They were called *Madeleines* and I'd discovered them a few weeks earlier. The label on the packaging described them as buttery treats. Since there wasn't a calorie count listed, I chose to assume they were calorie free.

We'd each had two when Diane got around to the major reason for her visit. She pulled a plastic evidence bag from her purse. I could see a bloody cell phone inside. My appetite vanished.

"We've downloaded all the digital data from Margo Cager's phone. My partner thinks you might be able to get something off it that we can't through conventional means. Want to give it a try? The Scarsdale police found the phone in the sweater Margo was wearing when she died. They let me borrow it for a few hours so I could show it to you."

I stared at the bag. I really didn't want to see Margo's last minutes but the detective was right about one thing, the body count was rising. I reached out a hand and took it.

***

The plastic bag was interfering, but I wasn't keen on doing it anyway. I could barely hear Margo's voice. She was arguing with someone.

"Anything?" Diane's voice was filled with impatience and skepticism

I ignored her. I wrapped both hands around the plastic bag, squeezing it hard.

Margo was in a parked car. I could see her sitting in the driver's seat, looking at an apartment building.

"You've had your warning. By now you should know my associates are serious. We're done discussing this." Margo's voice came through loud and clear. "You know what I need. I've told you what I'll pay for it. We had a deal. Don't even think about screwing me over on the price or the next time you won't get your 'son' back. Just remember I know your secret and the next time you fail to deliver, the police are going to know too."

"Val? Val?"

I opened my eyes. "She was threatening someone. She wanted them to buy something for her or maybe...."

"Maybe what?" Maybe I didn't know Margo at all.

"When is a carjacking not really a carjacking?"

***

I hung up the phone and rolled over, trying to nap. At my insistence Diane had checked the list of contacts and calls from Margo's cell phone. She had phoned to let me know that my latest theory was wrong. There was no record of Margo ever calling Alisha and Rudy Warren, Christopher's parents.

I still had a pounding headache and my psychic reading off of Margo's cell phone had drained me both physically and emotionally. In this case I was happy to be wrong. And it wasn't as if it was the first time my so-called talents had led me astray.

"Stop thinking about it. And you definitely don't need to tell Jake about it." I pulled Jake's pillow over my head to block the late afternoon light.

Using an old trick, I pulled up a childhood memory and focused on it until I fell asleep.

"Valentine, my mother, your great grandmother, had the sight like you. You've been given a wonderful gift but you have to be careful how you use it. You'll discover that some people won't understand. Sometimes you won't understand."

"So if I hold the teacher's pencil and see the answers to a test, I shouldn't look?"

My grandmother's laughter filled my head. "Honey, you can look, you're only human. Just remember though that those answers might not be to *your* test."

Chapter 16

I couldn't believe we were returning to the scene of the crime, even if no one else but Jake and I knew that a crime had been committed. We were back on the Cross County, headed to Newton548's house. I'd have to remember to call him Stan Freedman instead of his online handle, especially since there was now another Newton548 haunting the Internet.

"Let's go over this one more time."

That was Jake's preschool teacher voice. The one he used when he was giving me instructions and wasn't convinced that I was going to follow them. Although to be honest, I could be stubborn like a three-year-old.

"Can I tell you again that I think this is a dumb idea?" Maybe he would hear me now that I had said it at least 50 times. Half of those before breakfast when he'd first sprang this notion on me.

He waved me off. "Just tell me again what you're supposed to be looking for?"

I recited dutifully. "A notebook, legal pad, scraps of paper, anything that would give me Newton's eBay password."

Jake took his eyes off the road. "Don't forget the Family Bible."

"You honestly think that Mr. Freedman kept a list of his passwords in the Old Testament?"

"Maybe. If the old guy was worried he'd forget it, he probably stashed the list in several places."

"And you assume that the killer has the password and is posing as him online. Why?"

Jake shrugged. "This is a sicko. I don't understand why he is doing anything. I just want to access Newton's buy and sell record. Maybe then I'd know where he got the Chang screen and—"

"And what?"

Jake moved onto the ramp for the Mount Vernon exit. "And I don't know much more than that. I'm flying by the seat of my pants, Val. I've got to rely on what we can find out the old-fashioned way without the benefit of your superpowers since so far, they've crapped out and haven't revealed the killer or what he wants."

Sometimes my husband is an ass. "This from the man who is preying on a dead man's relatives based on some cryptic information he got from a ghost that no one but he can see or hear."

Jake had the good sense to turn beet red. "Touché, my love."

We pulled up in front of Newton548's house. No crime scene tape dangled in the wind because according to the cops, there had been no crime. Just a confused old man dying in a trash-filled house. A short, bald man in his early 40s was waiting for us on the porch.

"Mr. Cohen?"

Jake hustled up the path, me trailing behind. "Sorry for your loss Mr. Freedman."

"Call me Frank. I understand you knew my uncle? Thank you for your offer to separate the treasure from the trash. When we're ready to liquidate, we'll of course want to work with your company."

Jake shook his head. "No sir. I'd want you to get at least three estimates from reputable firms, mine one of them, before you make a decision as to who to use. I can give you some names and you can check them out."

Jake was being exactly the man I married when he was talking to Frank Freedman. Honest, almost to a fault. He wouldn't take advantage of this situation, at least not monetarily. I decided to forgive his crack about my abilities.

We walked into the house, navigating our way around stacks of books, newspapers that were months' old, and dirty dishes.

"You said your uncle kept most of his antiques stock in two rooms, the dining room and a bedroom upstairs? Val will start up there and I'll work in the dining room. If I remember correctly, you're planning to toss or donate most of the furniture unless there's something of particular value."

Frank glanced around the shabby, crowded living room. "Hard to imagine but five years ago when my Aunt was alive, this house was a showplace. They used to give these wonderful parties, host all the holidays. But once my Aunt died, Uncle Stan became a recluse. In the last year, I thought his mind was slipping. Begged him to move into this nice assisted living residence in Tuckahoe. He got angry with me for even suggesting it. The old guy spent more time on the damn computer with people he never met than with anyone in real life."

Jake nodded. "That's how I knew him. Bought a couple of pieces from him. Had he owned his own antique shop?"

Frank laughed. "Uncle Stan was an accountant. My Aunt was the antique-er. Loved the thrill of the hunt. When she got sick, he could show her stuff he found online. It wasn't quite the same, but the two of them would follow the online auctions, she'd tell him how high to go in the bidding, even had him sell some of the pieces she'd accumulated over the years."

"What was your Aunt's name?" I glanced at Jake and could see he was thinking the same thing.

"Frieda. He called her Freddy. They never had kids, but they used to raise standard poodles. Last one died about the same time that Aunt Freddy passed on."

"I think I'll go on upstairs and start the inventory. Which room?"

"First one on the right at the top of the stairs. Used to be the master bedroom. The last few years, Uncle Stan has been sleeping on the sofa in the living room. I thought maybe the stairs bothered him, but from the amount of stuff up there, he was getting around okay."

Frank and Jake headed into the dining room. I took a last look around the living room. I could sense the old memories of happier times, caught a glimpse of a younger Stan Freedman, arm around the shoulders of a beautifully dressed woman. The glances between the couple told me that his world revolved around her. No wonder Stan felt so alone when his wife died.

I started to head upstairs, but walked back to the dining room. "Did your Uncle have Wi-Fi? I tapped the laptop bag hanging over my shoulder. "I'm going to take photos and create a data base for the antiques then upload the information to our shop. It will make the whole process quicker and you'll end up with a comprehensive report."

"Thanks!" Frank nodded in response to my question about the Wi-Fi. "Use the *FreddieGuest* connection. Uncle Stan got cable about two years ago. I installed the router for the Internet service myself. Up until then, he'd had a desktop model and DSL. Complained the DSL slowed down his bidding. In fact he kept upping his speed."

Jake stifled a groan. Newton548, the late Stan Freedman, had definitely become Speedy Gonzales in his online bidding wars.

"Do you know the password?"

Frank smiled. "I told him to pick something easy to remember. He chose Newton548. A little weird, but he insisted he wouldn't forget it."

***

There were four bedrooms upstairs. I took a quick peek into all of them. The first was a medium-sized bedroom that appeared to be in good shape, if unused and very dusty. Guestroom. The second was much smaller and packed with items still in their original boxes. It appeared Uncle Stan or maybe Freddie liked the shopping channels and had a thing for small appliances. The third bedroom was tiny. It was filled almost floor to ceiling with plastic garbage sacks. Checking down the hallway for any signs of the nephew, I opened one of the sacks. Household utility bills, receipts, grocery lists, any and all kinds of paper that one could generate during a lifetime. I saw a medical bill dated 1979. I was seeing signs of paranoia or maybe the guy was just a hoarder. I didn't envy Frank. He was going to be spending months just sorting the contents of this room.

The bedroom that I was supposed to be searching was the master bedroom. There were paths between stacks of furniture, lamps, and some nice pieces of artwork. I found my way to the windows and pulled back the heavy curtains. Like the rest of the house, the windows didn't seem to have been cleaned since Mrs. Freedman died.

I pulled out my laptop, logged on to the Wi-Fi connection, and headed to the eBay web site. I tried to log in using Newton548 as the eBay screen name, but repeating the name as a password got me an error message. I tried Freedman, Frieda, Freddy, nothing worked.

I began to take an inventory of the objects in the room, hoping that, in the process, I'd also come across some piece of paper that would reveal the password. Despite Jake's assertion, there was no Bible in the room.

I had the list of items that he had sold to the Changs, but nothing in the room seemed to match. I took photos of most of the objects and was covered in dust for my efforts. There were two final boxes in the corner of the room, next to an old mahogany armoire. I checked inside, but it contained formal gowns and a full-length mink coat, with the embroidered name of Frieda Freedman on the satin lining. More and more I felt sorry for the lonely old man who couldn't bear to part with his wife's clothes.

"What the hell?"

I took the larger box over to the window to be sure that I'd read the address label correctly.

Ms. Margo Cager, 429 Rodham Road, Scarsdale, NY 10583.

The carton wasn't sealed. Inside was a clock. I didn't have the photo that Jake had shown me, but it certainly resembled the antique Nanking clock that Jake had intended to sell to the Changs. I took several photographs. I dug around inside the box and found a handwritten note, dated a week earlier, on what appeared to be a notepad from Stan Freedman's previous life as an accountant.

"Per your request. Please find the clock and supporting paperwork authenticating its antiquity. Deposit balance of payment as discussed previously."

He didn't sound like a confused old man at all.

The smaller box, also addressed to Margo, contained what I was fairly sure was the Qing Dynasty Canton Export Card Case, also originally intended for the Changs. Again, I took several photographs.

"Val, you almost finished?" Jake was calling me.

"Be right there."

I looked around the room one more time. I noticed a photograph of Frieda, smiling broadly, standing next to a gorgeous French Poodle. The dog had a better hairdo than I ever would have. Clearly hours had been spent brushing and poofing the dog's jet black coat. Her collar was studded with rhinestones. On the back of the photo was an inscription, Freddy and Babycakes, May, 1998. The handwriting was the same as on the note to Margo.

I returned to eBay and logged in as Newton548. For a password, I typed in "Babycakes"

Bingo. I was in.

"Val?" Jake was calling again. "Frank's got an appointment. We've got to go. We'll come back next week to finish up."

I logged off and headed downstairs, more confused than ever.

How did Newton548 know Margo Cager? Where did he get these two antiques? Why did he or she want them? And why didn't Margo ask Jake to find them for her? And of course, the big one: Did the killer want these antiques too? If so why didn't he take them when he killed Newton?

Too many questions; too few answers.

***

We left Frank Freedman with the agreement that we'd meet again at the house in a few days. Jake promised some rough estimates of the value of major pieces in his uncle's collection.

"Want to stop at the luncheonette? Those cannoli were to die for, pun intended." He winked.

"Thanks, but I don't need the calories and I need you to listen without being distracted by ricotta and fried dough."

Reluctantly he drove past Theresa's Luncheonette and pulled onto the highway. "Okay, I'm all ears."

"I've got good news and bad news."

Jake sighed. "Why does it always have to be both?"

I smiled. "That's life, my sweet baboo."

Jake took his eyes off the road long enough to send a glare my way. It didn't work. "Sweet baboo? Let's work on our terms of endearment, Snookums."

"Well, honeybear, which do you want first? News that will bring you joy or information that will rock your world, turn your socks inside out, and leave you doubting everything you ever knew?"

"Um, the good news please. I think marrying you rocked my world enough."

"You got it. The good news is I figured out the password for Newton's eBay account."

Jake whistled. "Impressive. What is it?"

"Babycakes."

He did a quick double take. "What?"

"Name of their late, beloved dog."

Jake took a deep breath. "Okay, tell me the bad news."

"How well did you know Margo Cager?"

He looked confused. "Why? What about her?"

"Just give me a little background. You were already colleagues when we got together, right?"

"Uh huh." He nodded. "Yeah. I've known Margo for at least 10 years. She was just starting her design business and I had just opened the shop. Her ex-husband's connections on Wall Street meant she skipped into the big time almost immediately. To a certain extent she took me along for the ride. And when her husband was a total bastard and screwed every skirt in his office, and things were tough with my mom, well we shared a lot of Jack Daniels and late nights. But we also had a lot of laughs too. I'll miss her, pain in the ass that she could be."

He looked sad. Damn, I felt like I was about to spill the beans about Santa Claus to a five-year-old.

"I found a couple of boxes up in the bedroom."

"What does that have to do with Margo?"

I hesitated. Maybe I was misreading the situation. Maybe there was an innocent explanation for everything.

"Come on Val, spit it out. What's going on?"

"The boxes contained what I'm fairly certain was the Nanking clock you had ordered for the Changs, as well as the Qing Dynasty Card Case."

Jake stared at me in disbelief for several seconds. Too long as our car swerved into the right lane, almost clipping a green Corolla. He overcompensated and we almost skidded against the highway barrier.

I screamed. "Jake, pay attention. This is our exit."

He focused on the road. His knuckles turned white with the death grip he had on the steering wheel.

When we were safely on the side streets in Seamont, he muttered, "What was Stan Freedman doing with those pieces? Think it was just a coincidence?"

Now came the rip-off the band-aid part. Fast, brutal, painful, but done.

"I think he wanted it for a special client of his."

"Who?" I sensed curiosity mixed with fear.

I put my hand on his arm. "The boxes were addressed to Margo at her home. Inside there was a memo from Stan to Margo, dated about a week ago, saying she should deposit the balance of the payment as agreed."

Jake pulled into our driveway. "What the hell is going on? Why would...."

He couldn't finish. I didn't blame him. I was sure that he felt confused and betrayed. He was staring straight ahead, almost in a trance.

I didn't have a clue what it all meant either. "Maybe we should call Diane. Tell her of the connection between

Margo and Newton, er Stan. Maybe this is getting too complicated and we need to back out?"

He didn't answer. Just kept staring out the windshield.

"Val?" His voice soft, tense.

"Right here, sweetheart. Let's go in. I'll make some tea."

"Call the Seamont police." His voice was stronger. "Call them right now."

"Okay." I dug my cell phone out of my purse. "I'll leave a message for Diane if she's not there. No point in talking to Mike Hardesty. He's nice, but–"

"Tell them to send a squad car immediately."

"Why?"

He pointed out the front windshield. "There."

My VW convertible was parked in the driveway were I'd left it. But it was now permanently open to the elements. The top had been shredded, probably with a big knife.

CHAPTER 17

"Guess Richard didn't go to Canada."

Diane blushed but didn't say anything in response. She was still writing up her incident report, sitting at my kitchen table. Jake was on the phone with our insurance agent.

"If you'll just sign here," Diane said, pointing to the blank line at the bottom of the multi-page form. "We still have the APB out on him. My partner is getting a search warrant issued right now. He's going to interview Javier Baez again and search his home and business. If we find anything at all, we'll arrest the old man and hope that brings in the son."

"I don't think Javier knows anything." I poured three cups of tea. "I feel sorry for him, his son has obviously gone off the deep end."

Diane pointed again to the report.

I put the teapot down and signed it, not that I thought it was going to do me any good. But Jake would need a copy in order to file a claim. This was going to be a lot more expensive than replacing a tire.

"Yeah, well, we all have at least one family member who's short a few marbles, but they don't usually go around threatening people and vandalizing cars. Javier Baez knows something. His son didn't get this way overnight."

Her statement reminded me of Newton548 and his nephew. I still couldn't decide if Stan had all his facilities or not. He obviously had enough marbles left to do business with Margo. Now I had to wonder if that got him killed.

Jake finally got off the phone and joined us at the table.

He took a sip of tea and pointed at the form. "I need a copy."

"The green one is yours." She tore the last page off and left it on the table. She put the worn form pad back in her jacket pocket.

The television came on in the living room, the voice of the host of a popular cooking show startling all of us.

"Who–"

Jake answered Diane before she could get the question out. "I think someone's garage door opener is tuned to the same frequency as our television remote. I'm going to have to buy a new remote. Or maybe a new television. One of those 50 inch–"

"Forget it," I said. "We have a new furnace to pay for. Just unplug the tv when we're not using it."

We both knew there was nothing wrong with the television. Jake's mother liked to pop in and watch the *Barefoot Contessa*. Neither of us wanted to introduce her to Diane.

Jake glanced at me. I nodded.

"I'll go turn it off." I picked up the incident report and walked towards the living room, intending to put the form on Jake's desk for safekeeping on my way back. I didn't even make it out of the kitchen.

As I held the form I heard Diane's voice in my head. I shut my eyes and she was standing in our driveway next to my vandalized car, talking on her cell phone to Chief Peterson.

"We might have gotten a break. We found a knife in the Cohen car. Looks like one of those old Chinese knives.

It could be the murder weapon in the Berman case, maybe Margo Cager's too. Hardesty is bringing it in. We need it checked for prints right away."

The Chief's answer was too low for me to hear. Something about searching our house.

Shocked, I dropped the paper to the carpet but not before I heard Diane say that Jake was still their prime suspect for all the murders.

***

Detective Ellison—and she was Detective Ellison in my mind again—offered to walk through our house, make sure all the windows and doors were secure. Secure my ass! I firmly declined her kind offer before Jake could answer. He probably thought I was worried about his mother. She was the least of our problems. The police were still lying to us, pretending to follow the leads we gave them, when all the while they were concentrating their investigation on Jake.

I showed her out, firmly locking the door behind her.

"What's going on?" Jake asked, walking down the stairs into the foyer.

"Where's your mother?"

"Upstairs. I told her she could spend the night. She's worried about us."

"She's got cause. The police are lying to us. They found an antique Chinese knife in the VW."

"A Chinese–"

"Yes. Apparently it's a match to the one they found at the Bermans' murder scene."

Jake frowned. "They never said anything about finding a knife."

"I know." I tugged him towards the stairs. "The knife was one of those things they were holding back, a way to identify the real killer."

"How did you find–"

"Never mind that now. I think the police are going to be coming back with a search warrant for our house."

"Why? Searching for what?"

"When we relocated merchandise from the shop I saw a pair of Chinese knives."

Jake shook his head. "Not a pair, I have a set of three. I purchased them for–"

"Let me guess, the Changs?"

"Yeah, but no one knew about them. Not even the Changs. They were relatively cheap and I purchased them on-line thinking they were something the Changs might like. Instead the Changs were killed and I forgot about the knives for months. Never did find a buyer. They've been gathering dust in a display case ever since."

"Wait. How many did you say you bought?"

"Three. I thought the Changs might put them in a shadow box, next to the screen."

"When was the last time you saw them?"

Jake shrugged. "When I cleaned everything in the display case a month or two ago."

"And you cleaned three?"

"Yes, Val, I cleaned three Chinese knives and put them back in the case."

He still didn't get it.

"And you haven't looked at them since."

Jake nodded.

"We need to find them. Right now." I ran down the hall. Jake right behind me.

My memory was that I'd put the pair of knives along with some small items in a cardboard box on the kitchen table.

I had a sick feeling that we were only going to find one in the box. Worse still Jake's fingerprints were going to be on the two the police had and the one still in our house. Someone was setting Jake up to take the fall for the Bermans and Margo. And they were doing a very good job.

***

"What happened to the other two knives?"

For a very smart guy, Jake was still several beats behind on what was happening.

I sighed. "I think I know."

"You've got a vision of..."

I shook my head. "No visions, no premonitions. Like you, I'm being swept along by this avalanche of horror with no forewarnings."

Jake rolled his eyes. "So what good are your visions, then?"

For a guy who was about to be arrested on first degree murder charges, he was either naïve or clueless, or both.

"Jake, be serious. Someone used one of those knives to viciously murder the Bermans, probably to kill Margo as well."

"No." His voice was barely a whisper.

His face went sheet white. He sank down on a kitchen chair like all the air had been let out of his body.

I grabbed the remaining knife and stuck it in my purse. "We've got to get rid of this, pronto."

Jake just stared into space.

"I'll drive over to Red Bridge and toss it into the Sound."

"Who hates me that much?" He looked like a little kid who didn't understand the spanking he'd just gotten.

"Jake. Concentrate. We'll figure out the who and why later. Right now, I've got to dump this knife."

"Doesn't matter." His voice was so soft I had to strain to hear it.

I put on my coat. "We don't want them to find it here."

Jake grabbed my arm. "My fingerprints are all over those knives. I didn't wear gloves when I polished them.

Whether or not they find the third one in my house doesn't much matter."

He had a point.

"Wait. You have an alibi for the night the Bermans were killed."

He smiled. "You're my alibi. I was asleep next to you, but I doubt you stayed up all night watching me, not that the word of a devoted wife is much help."

"I always wake up when you get out of bed," I protested. "I absolutely would know if you'd snuck out of the house."

He squeezed my hand. "That's not what I'd call an ironclad alibi, but I appreciate the thought. The problem is motive. Why would I want to kill the Bermans?"

"Or Margo or Newton," I added.

His eyes narrowed. "Nah, I can think of reasons to kill Margo and Newton. They were competitors and I hate to be outbid. It's the Bermans that make no sense. Unless…"

Now I was confused. "Unless what?"

Jake got up and started pacing. "Unless it was to cover up the reason for killing the Changs."

I threw up my hands. "So now you've murdered six people?"

"Well, if you buy the logic of me as the killer, then it all goes back to the Changs, everything follows from that."

I thought about that for a few moments. "Okay. Here's what we know. Alex Fletcher is in prison for murdering the Changs, but he didn't do it."

"But that's on your say-so," Jake objected. "They had the evidence to convict him."

"They're wrong. I knew it five years ago. But in any case, he sure didn't kill the Bermans, Newton, or Margo."

Jake nodded. "So the cops are going to say that I decided to be a copycat killer. Follow the example Fletcher set. Except for Newton who they are sure wasn't murdered at all."

"What else do we know for sure?"

"Nothing." Jake shrugged. "Lots of theories,"–he smiled at me–"and a vision or two."

"Okay, maybe my visions aren't admissible in court, but they're at least a place to start. We need to find Christopher's parents."

"Christopher? Our Christopher?" At my smile, he blushed. "The baby we saved from the carjacking?"

I nodded. "I wasn't going to tell you because I wasn't sure...I'm still not sure...but Margo may have threatened the parents. They could be in danger. I remember at the hospital the police told me their names were Alisha and Rudy Warren. Let's start there. They live in an apartment house in Queens."

CHAPTER 18

"How long do you think it will take the police to get a search warrant for our house?" Jake asked. His fingers were nervously clutching the steering wheel.

The traffic into Queens was bad. It felt like we were about making about 15 miles an hour downhill with the wind behind our backs, less on the straightaways. At this rate Christopher could be starting first grade before we arrived.

"No idea. However long it takes to get a warrant. I might have worked for lawyers before we got married, but they didn't share a lot of the nuts and bolts with me. Maybe tomorrow morning." I turned on the overhead light for a quick glance at my watch. It was about 8:30. "They could be at the house right now."

"I told my mother to get out of town. But she usually doesn't listen to me. They might get more than they bargained for."

I smiled at the thought of Ruth Cohen giving Detective Ellison a piece of her mind. Ruth wouldn't tolerate the police tearing up what she still considered her home.

"Val?"

"Yeah?"

"Not that I don't believe you but is there any chance that your vision, what you saw and heard was out of context?"

"Not this time. At least not the part about you being the prime suspect and that they were going to get a search warrant to look for more knives."

"I have to tell you Valentine that the next time the police come knocking at our door for help, I might actually commit murder and it won't be with an antique weapon."

I had the remaining Chinese knife in my purse. Maybe tossing it off a bridge was a bad idea, but leaving it in the house wasn't an option. The killer didn't need a third knife to plant at his next murder scene. And best case, keeping it out of police hands might delay them a few days. After all Jake bought and sold a large number of antiques. The fact his fingerprints were on antique knives used by a murder didn't conclusively tie him to the murders. The district attorney would need more for an indictment. We needed to make sure he didn't get it.

Jake sighed. "Why would Margo threaten Christopher's parents? How did she know them?"

"I don't know. I told you I wasn't sure I had that part right. The police didn't find any connection between them, or at least none that they told me about. For all I know the police didn't even check. But the least we can do is warn the Warrens that a killer may be after them."

We used the rest of the drive to silently contemplate our fate.

Or at least that's what I assumed Jake was thinking about. I was certainly scrambling to put the pieces together. Someone was killing in order to find something or multiple somethings. I'd always felt that the killer hated the Changs. I might have gotten that wrong. Maybe the killer's emotions were different from normal people's. Maybe his frustration manifested itself as hate. I'd just read him, read the murder scene wrong. What else had I read wrong? Margo? Her phone? What had I really seen and what had I just assumed?

Jake made a turn and suddenly we were getting close. "Start looking for a parking space."

"You know after thinking about it, I realize I was reading Margo's phone not because of a telephone call Margo made using it, but because the phone was with her all the time. Kind of like Diane Ellison's police incident report pad. Or that lipstick one of the Berman daughters dropped."

"You should practice speed reading," Jake joked. "You just keep getting bits and pieces. I could have used some more information from Diane about my upcoming arrest."

"Hey, I wasn't prepared to do a touch reading and panicked a little when I heard Diane's voice in my head." I pointed towards the brake lights on a parked car that just flickered on. "First time I've ever gotten that much off of a document without trying. I wish I'd held onto the report a little longer. I can't believe that woman lied to me again. Remind me to burn that bridge so I don't walk over it again. You are all the *friend* I need. Everyone else lies to me."

Jake pulled the Tahoe into the open spot and turned off the motor. "Maybe we could talk about getting a dog again. Dogs make great friends."

Dogs? Something was at the back of my mind. Something about dogs. "Margo had Heidi, at least part-time. What about the Bermans? Did they have a dog? Newton548 had a poodle."

"Val, I don't want a poodle or a greyhound. I thought maybe we could just go to a shelter and adopt a mutt."

"Jake, we're on the run from the police. Now isn't the time to acquire a pet. I just want to know if dogs are another connection between the victims."

"Right, we'll have to check on the Bermans." He grinned. "But when this is all over, if I'm not in jail, I won't forget you didn't say a definite *no* to getting a dog."

***

"Are you sure this is the right address?"

"Obviously not."

We were looking around inside an empty apartment. The building manager had said the apartment was empty. He'd gone on to say the last tenant was a little old lady with a cat. A sick cat. He was happy to see her go after the cat died. And for twenty bucks he was happy to show the apartment to us.

"Who told you this was the Warrens' address?"

I sighed. "The hospital. This is the address the emergency room doctor gave me when I called him yesterday."

"I thought doctors weren't supposed to give out personal information about their patients to the public," Jake said, frowning. "That's illegal."

"Oh he didn't give it out. Not to the public. He gave it to the health insurance company representative who was handling the hospital's reimbursement claim. Totally different thing."

Jake chuckled. "And that representative was you?"

"Yep. Helps to have had an aunt who worked for Blue Cross and Blue Shield for forty years until she retired last year. You pick up the lingo."

"Well, either the doctor's records were wrong or the Warrens lied about where they lived."

I walked into the kitchen and opened a cabinet. "Why would they lie about where they lived?"

"Maybe they couldn't pay the hospital bill." Jake picked up a yellowed slip of paper sticking out from under a closet door. "The old lady, her name was Anna Sizemore, had overdue vet bills. That cat had kidney problems. $700 for some procedure. Another reason to have dogs."

"You're reaching."

"I am. But I'm getting anxious. The police could be ransacking our house right now. Can you sense anything?"

"About our house? Get real."

"No, about this apartment?"

I sniffed. "Yeah, the old lady didn't change the kitty litter often enough."

***

We were back in the basement, talking to Franco, the building manager. "You interested in the apartment? I got somebody else who left me a deposit, but if you want it...."

I suspected Franco had checked out Jake's Tahoe and wanted to see if we might want to offer him an incentive to lose the paperwork of the other renter.

"I don't think it meets our needs," Jake said, taking another $20 bill from his wallet. "Did a young couple with a baby ever live in the building? Baby is about 8 months old. "

Franco snatched the bill out of Jake's hand. "Nope. Ain't had a squalling brat in this building in at least 10 years."

"Do you have the address of Anna Sizemore, the woman who used to rent the apartment?"

Franco looked at Jake and waited. He snatched the next $20 bill before answering.

"She moved in with her daughter. They live on Utopia Parkway. Daughter's name is Marsha. Never married. Wasn't much of a looker, but had a set of...." He winked at Jake.

I felt dirty just listening.

Jake grabbed my hand and headed up the dark stairwell to the outer door. "Thanks for your time."

Franco called after us. "If you change your mind about the apartment, call me."

"I'd live on a bench in Central Park before...."

Jake wasn't listening. He was running a search on his phone for Marsha Sizemore's address.

"Got it. Let's go."

I checked my watch. It was almost nine o'clock. "Maybe it's too late."

Jake pulled into traffic. "Time may be running out for Christopher and his parents. We'll drive by and if the lights are on, we'll ring the doorbell."

I checked his face. He was really worried about that little baby. He'd bonded with Christopher even more than I realized, probably more than even he knew. Plus Jake's biological clock was ticking too. A dog would be good, but it was a baby, his baby, he wanted.

Mrs. Sizemore hadn't moved far from her old neighborhood. Her daughter's address was definitely a little more upscale, or at least a little less shabby. She lived in the bottom half of a duplex, which conveniently for us, was fully lit up.

Jake was out of the car before I could even release my seatbelt. I hustled to catch up with him.

"What are you going to say?" It hadn't seemed to have occurred to my husband that unlike Franco who was more than willing to trade information for money, the Sizemores might have a few more ethics.

"Just follow along," Jake hissed, ringing the doorbell.

I could hear shuffling and then a querulous, "Who's there?"

"Mrs. Sizemore? My name is Jake Cohen. I'm looking for Alisha and Rudy Warren. They have a little baby named Christopher."

The door opened a smidgen. The security door chain firmly in place. I could see an elderly, suspicious face peering out.

"I don't know anybody named Christopher Warner."

"No ma'am. The parents' names are Alisha and Rudy Warren. Their baby is named Christopher. I think they're in danger." Jake spoke slowly. He took out his cell phone, skimmed through some stored photos, and held one up to Mrs. Sizemore. I had no idea that he'd taken a photo of Christopher in the hospital.

A thin bony hand snaked through the narrow opening and snatched Jake's phone. I could see the old woman bring the photo up close to her face. After a few moments, she gave the phone back and without a word, closed the door.

Jake and I exchanged glances. Another dead end I thought, until I heard the door chain slide along the track and the door open.

"Come in. My daughter is out. She wouldn't like me having people in, but I recognized the baby. You say he's in danger?"

Jake nodded. "I think so."

Anna Sizemore, dressed in a worn, purple housecoat, hairnet covering her grey pincurls, and clutching a walker, shuffled into the adjoining sitting room. We followed. With effort, she sat down on an ugly red and gold brocade loveseat, looking totally out of place in her daughter's modern living room. We perched on matching club chairs.

"I love to look at baby pictures. Always hoped I'd have some of my own grandchildren's photos to share, but Marsha, that's my daughter, she never married. Got a good job with the city government, but a paycheck isn't something you can show to other grandmothers."

She looked so sad, but I worried her daughter would come back, so I pushed on. "Did the Warrens live near you?"

She looked confused. "Live nearby? Do they live in Queens too?"

Jake interrupted. "Maybe. We're trying to find them. Do you have their address?"

"Heavens, no. Why would I know where they lived? I don't know anyone named Warren."

Jake and I exchanged glances. Maybe Mama Sizemore was just a lonely old lady who wanted company."

I thought I'd give it one more shot. "So you don't know where we can find Christopher or his parents?"

"No, I'm sorry. I have no idea where that cute baby lives. I wish I could be more help."

Jake and I walked to the front door, Mrs. Sizemore shuffling behind us.

Ever the polite man I married, Jake smiled at the elderly lady. "Thank you for your time. Be sure and lock the door behind us."

Mrs. Sizemore offered a small grin. "I'm not even going to tell Marsha I had company."

The door closed behind us; the security chain slid into place. We were almost down the front steps when the door opened again.

"Do you have a cat?" Mrs. Sizemore walked slowly out on the front porch. A wind ruffled her hairnet.

"No, ma'am."

Her housecoat was thin and the old woman shivered. I knew she'd like a longer visit, but we had to get home. "It's cold, Mrs. Sizemore You should get back inside."

"I miss Belle. That was my cat. She'd curl up next to me and keep me warm."

I didn't know what to do. The elderly woman seemed lost. Under other circumstances, I'd have waited with her until her daughter came home, but that would surely cause a big argument between the two of them. I tried again. "Please Mrs. Sizemore, go inside before you get sick."

The old woman nodded. "I just thought if you had a cat you should know that they take fine care of them at East Village Veterinary Hospital. Marsha thought I was foolish to take my Belle into the city, but that was the best place for her when Belle got sick. You had to wait a long time to see the vet, but I'd sit there, Belle on my lap, and chat with the other people in the waiting room, get to see the pictures of their grandkids. I wish I'd had some pictures to show. Sometimes I'd show photos of one of my cousin's grandkids, but it wasn't the same."

My heart started racing. "Is that where you saw Christopher's photo?"

Mrs. Sizemore nodded. "One of the assistants, I don't know his name, was showing the ladies behind the desk pictures of his little boy. He let me look too. Such a pretty baby."

A cold wind whipped through the front porch. Jake put his arm around the bony shoulders of the old woman. "Let's get you back inside."

I followed them, stopping once near the door to look back over my shoulder. There was a darkness out there that had nothing to do with the night.

CHAPTER 19

"We probably should have gone home," Jake mused, staring up at the ceiling of the hotel room. "Taking off like that makes us look guilty."

I sat down on the bed next to him and tried to towel dry my hair. "My hair is going to frizz. There was only about a teaspoon full of–"

"Valentine, you're avoiding the subject. We're fugitives from justice. Our faces may be on post office walls before the week is out!"

"Do they even do that anymore? I mean with the Internet and everything? Anyway, who stands around the post office and looks at the walls?"

"I'm surprised we haven't gotten a call from your friend Diane, trying to track us down. Or spinning some lie to get us to come to them."

"She's not my friend." I leaned over and dried the underside of my hair. "But that reminds me. Turn off your cell phone and take out the battery so they can't track us down."

"Oh, hell and damnation!" He jumped up and grabbed his phone from a pocket of the jacket he'd hung over the desk chair. "That's why I never wanted to carry a cell phone. I was the one who warned you about satellites tracking people using cell phones! I should have remembered to do this before we left home."

"Relax, Jake. They probably won't think we're on the run until at least tomorrow. We've got a couple of days before the cell phone company gives up our records. It's not like we're suspected terrorists or anything. We're just run-of-the-mill serial killers."

"I don't know why you are joking about this. Val, we need a lawyer and I don't know where the money is going to come from. Maybe you could get a vision about that!" He stalked into the bathroom and slammed the door.

"There's always your second cousin Dwight!"–My voice was too loud for the thin walls of the cheap hotel, but I didn't care–"I hear he finally passed the bar last year." I wadded up the towel and threw it across the room towards the bathroom. It dropped soundlessly in a damp heap on the carpet and offered me no satisfaction.

Jake opened the door and stuck out his head. "Dwight is a pompous, glue-sniffing, imbecile. And those are just his good points."

I walked over and picked up the towel. Leaning against the bathroom doorway, I watched Jake use the complimentary toothbrush to clean his teeth. He had already done that twice since we'd checked in. He was angry and well on his way to blaming me for the situation we found ourselves in.

"Your mother said that glue-sniffing was just a one-time thing he did in high school."

He rinsed his mouth and spit into the sink. "My mother doesn't know everything."

"I always suspected that." I couldn't help grinning. "It will be our little secret."

"Right." He took the towel from me and dried his face. "So tomorrow we go visit the vet?"

I wrapped my arms around him. "First thing."

***

The address in Manhattan's East Village was high-priced, super cool, and incredibly frustrating. We'd been driving around and around and around looking for a parking place, because my husband hates to pay for parking garages. He would have had better luck winning the New York Powerball than finding a legal street parking spot. I'd have thought the possibility of getting arrested for multiple murders might have been an incentive for him to throw the car into an overpriced parking lot. But I would have been wrong. I was getting carsick and wanted out of my husband's beloved Tahoe. Enough was enough.

"Pull in there." I pointed to a garage squeezed in between two apartment houses.

"They'll scratch the Tahoe," he grumbled, but he did pull in. The garage was two blocks away from the animal hospital. $25 an hour or any fraction thereof. If we stayed on the run much longer we were going to have to find an ATM.

***

We hustled through the narrow streets, crowded with people rushing to work, kids on their way to school, and loads of dog walkers commandeering the width of the sidewalk with their furry charges tugging on their leashes.

Jake had refused to plan a script for our visit to the animal hospital. He'd climbed into bed, punched the pillow into submission, and pretended to fall asleep so he didn't have to talk to me. But with just a half block to go, I felt like it was past time to push the point. "So how are we playing this? You meet Rudy Warren and just announce that he and his family are in grave danger?"

"Something like that." He held open the door to the animal hospital. Despite the fancy address, there is a common smell and look to all vet offices. Even with the best disinfectants, the smell of cats, dogs, and urine lingers in the air. The worn linoleum floor was evidence of hundreds of paws that had walked across it. The waiting room was already crowded with men and women, holding their beloved four-legged family members.

Jake headed directly for the long reception desk where two young women were working.

"I hope you can help me. I'm looking for Rudy Warren. I understand he works here."

A plump girl in her 20s, Megan by her name tag, looked up from her computer. "Is your pet a patient here?"

"No. I don't have any animals, at least not yet, but I need to see Rudy Warren."

I could hear the urgency in Jake's voice and see the distrust in Megan's eyes.

Megan shook her head and turned her eyes back to her computer screen. "I'm sorry. We're busy. You'll need to make an appointment."

Jake leaned across the desk and Megan pushed her chair back.

"You don't understand. This is literally a matter of life and death. I won't take much of his time, but I've got to see Rudy Warren. Now."

Jake's voice was loud enough to set off a cacophony of barking amongst the waiting room group.

The other receptionist stood up and walked over to us. "Keep your voice down or I'm calling the cops."

I could see that Jake was rapidly unspooling. I put my hand on his. "Forgive my husband Jake. He's terribly worried about Rudy Warren's little boy, Christopher. Jake is the one who rescued the baby when the Warrens' car was stolen with Christopher inside. Did Rudy tell you about it? I think it was in the newspapers."

Megan and the other receptionist exchanged glances.

"Rudy Warren doesn't work here anymore." Megan said flatly.

"When…when did he leave?" Jake gripped the edge of the reception desk.

Megan shrugged. "He didn't show up for work three days ago. We called his cell phone, but it had been disconnected. The emergency number we had, I think it was his wife's, was also disconnected. Sorry, but I've got no idea where Rudy Warren is. If he's expecting a decent reference, he's gonna have to look elsewhere. The docs are really pissed. He totally left us in the lurch. We're all having to cover his shifts."

I squeezed Jake's hand. He had the worst poker face. His disappointment and fear were almost palpable.

There was one last place to look. "Do you have Rudy's home address?"

Megan checked her computer. "Yes, but I'd bet he isn't there."

"Still, if you have it, it would help ease our minds if we could just swing by and check. Maybe his neighbors know how we can get in touch."

She wrote out the address and slid it across the desk.

Jake picked it up and I didn't think his face could get any paler, but it did. Beads of sweat appeared on his forehead. His breath got faster, harsher.

I looked at the address. 598 Newton Street, Mt. Vernon, NY, a half block from Stan Freedman's house.

***

We sat in the Tahoe parked across the street from the Warrens' address. It was an apartment over the top of a boarded-up store—a bakery if the faded signs on the front were to be believed. The truth was, we didn't know what to believe anymore.

"Okay, the plan is the same as before? Basically, no plan?" I didn't like the feel of this place. Maybe it was because it was so close to Stan Freedman's house. I wanted nothing more than to tell Jake we should go home, hire a lawyer, and take our chances with the legal system. But my timing was off, now Jake was the one determined to find out how the Chang murders of five years ago were linked to the deaths of the Bermans, Margo, and Stan Freedman.

A feeling of dread sank over me as we entered the narrow stairway to the apartment. I said a silent prayer that we were ahead of the killer and that the Warrens were still alive.

Jake rang the bell.

No one came to the door.

He knocked. When there was no response, he tried the door. It was locked.

Glancing at me, he pointed towards the doorknob. "Want to give it a go?"

Reluctantly, I placed a hand on the doorknob and closed my eyes, trying to get some kind of reading. I concentrated on clearing my mind and listening. There was nothing.

After a few minutes Jake nudged me. "Anything?"

"No. Do you think we should try to get a look inside?"

He frowned. "How? There's a dead bolt. We're not getting in this way. And unless you've developed wings, we're not dropping down from the roof and looking through a window."

"Do you think there is an entrance through the store? It's an old building. Maybe the apartment was originally the shop owner's home."

Jake groaned. "Fine. Let's check it out. I guess a murderer shouldn't have any qualms about breaking and entering."

***

We went in through a back door to the bakery fairly easily, the lock having been jimmied in the past by someone else determined to get inside without a key. I had to wonder how far in the past that might have been? Ten years or ten minutes?

I didn't voice that fear to Jake. Instead I asked, "What if there's a security alarm?"

"Valentine, I doubt they would pay for something like that and leave a door in this condition."

Right. Assuming that whoever "they" were knew about the door.

The bakery kitchen was empty of anything food related. It smelled damp. I'd bet money the building had a mold problem. And a mouse infestation. There were droppings all over the worn linoleum floor. Apparently the structure was being used for storage. There were dozens of opened wooden crates. Pink Styrofoam worms spilled out everywhere.

I dug around in one crate and snagged a stuffed panda bear. I stuck my hand in again and pulled out another identical bear, the sleeve of my jacket covered with the static-charged worms.

Jake checked another crate. "China dolls over here. I doubt any of them are antiques. Wonder who owns this merchandise. The Warrens? Maybe they were going to reopen this store as a toy shop. Stay here, I'm going to get a flashlight out of the Tahoe. The power is off and we're going to need some more light if only to scare off the rodent population. I'm also going to move the Tahoe over to the next block. We don't want to alert anyone that we're in here."

With everything that had happened to us I knew better than to argue that his actions bordered on paranoia. I nodded my agreement with his plan and tossed the bear back in the crate. I looked into another, a larger one. It measured about four feet by three feet and was about three feet tall. Even in the dim light, I could see it was almost empty. Most of the worms had escaped, but about a dozen shrink-wrapped books remained in the bottom. I pulled one out. It was a world atlas, the oversized kind you could still see in libraries but that no one used any more with the advent of the Internet.

I carried the book with me and wandered out of the kitchen and into the main room where the light was better. I was just going to take a quick peek around while I waited for Jake. There was a door to my left. Opening it, I found the stairs to the apartment. "Well, I got one thing right at least."

Turning to go back to the kitchen, I heard a rustling sound behind me, then there was crushing pain in the back of my head. I dropped the atlas. My world went black.

***

I woke to a sense of motion and the worst headache I'd ever had in my life. I was lying on my side, my knees almost to my chest. I tried to open my eyes, but something was covering them. Besides a blindfold, it felt like there was some kind of bag over my head. There was tape over my mouth. Tape around my ankles.

When I tried to bring my hands to my face, I discovered they were tied behind my back.

I fought the panic that was threatening to overwhelm me. There wasn't enough air. I stretched out my legs and hit something. Given the sense of movement, I guessed I was in the back seat of a car.

I started kicking whatever I could reach, the door, the back of the front seat, making guttural noises since I couldn't speak.

"Knock it off, bitch or I'll toss you in the trunk. No heat back there."

I didn't recognize the male voice.

The car made a sharp right turn and headed down what felt like a gravel road. After about ten minutes it stopped so abruptly that I was tossed off the seat and landed on the floor. There was a blast of cold air as someone opened the back door, cut the tape on my ankles, and hauled me out, forcing me to walk across what felt like concrete, then along a wooden walkway. I heard a key turn, a door open, and suddenly I was shoved into a confined space. The bag over my head was removed and the tape across my mouth was ripped off. The blindfold remained.

"Sit down." Heavy hands forced me to the floor.

"Who are you? What do you want?" I couldn't get the words out fast enough. With a sob I couldn't control, I added, "Please don't hurt me." Damn, I hated the way my voice sounded, pitiful, weak, but I was petrified. My premonition in the Fletcher murder trial courtroom–was this the event?

He grabbed my hair and yanked it. I let out a scream and he backhanded my face.

"Shut up. You and your husband have caused enough trouble. Just tell me where it is and I'll leave you alone."

I tried to control my sobs. "I don't know what you want."

He slapped me again. "Don't toy with me."

I gasped, sparks flashed behind my eyes and the contents of my stomach rose. I took a deep breath, trying to ignore the pain in my head.

Despite my best efforts I threw up, I could hear the splatter on the floor.

My kidnapper was not pleased, but despite the ensuing string of curses, I sensed him stepping back from me.

I tilted my head and wiped my mouth on the upper arm of my jacket, "Look, I'm not lying. I don't know what you're looking for. You can have anything we own. Do you want money? We don't have a lot, but Jake will give you whatever he has."

There was a mirthless laugh. "You think you can buy me off with a few thousand? I've invested years in this search. What do you take me for? It's the millions I'm after."

I heard him move closer and I started crying, ducking my head to avoid another slap. I'd never been hit before and I really didn't like it.

"Please, listen to me. I don't know who told you we were rich, but we've got nothing but the house and we've got a mortgage on that. But Jake will go to the bank...."

"Shut up, bitch. Maybe I should have grabbed your husband. He'll know where that last piece is."

The kidnapper grabbed my hair and forced my head back. I could smell his sweat, his breath was stinking. He whispered in my ear. "You'd better pray that your husband will fork it over if he ever hopes to see his precious bride again."

Suddenly I heard the door open, then slam shut. I could hear a lock being thrown, and I was alone in the dark.

CHAPTER 20

I think I passed out again. When I regained consciousness I was shaking from the cold and I desperately needed to rinse my mouth. On the plus side the pain in my head had faded to a bearable level.

I also appreciated the fact I was still alive.

But for how much longer? If my kidnapper was the man who'd killed at least six people, maybe more, then I probably wouldn't survive his next visit.

How much time had passed? How long had he been gone?

I managed to sit up. My hands were tied tightly, but in front of me now. I could feel that my wedding ring was gone.

Once vertical the nausea returned with a vengeance. I threw up again, mostly dry heaves this time. I felt dizzy. My thoughts were scattered.

Wherever I was, it wasn't heated. More snow was forecast. The cold could easily kill me. The killer probably wouldn't come back if Jake gave him what he wanted. But the chances of Jake having what the guy wanted was doubtful. If the killer came back it would be to finish me off.

I needed to save myself. No one was going to do it for me.

Deliberately, I slowed my breathing down and counted to ten. I needed to clear my head and think logically. Being able to see would be an immense help.

I fumbled to get my hands up to my eyes. My fingers felt wooden and could barely bend. But I tugged at the fabric around my eyes. I managed to push it up onto my forehead. It took a few moments for my eyes to adjust. I needed something to lean against to stop the spinning; something stationary to anchor me in the blackness.

I rocked backwards, scooting on my bottom across the floor. It seemed to take forever before I felt a rough wooden wall behind me.

Finally, I could see light seeping under and above the door to my cell. Okay, it wasn't a cell. But it was much smaller than I'd assumed. About the size of a walk-in closet.

I rested a minute. The effort of moving a few feet had exhausted me and my head pounded. I wanted to drift off to sleep, but I knew if I did, I'd die.

I didn't want to die just yet. I began to speak aloud to keep awake and focused.

"What's next Valentine?"

"My hands. I need to get my hands untied."

"Hurry."

"I can't. I need something to cut the tape."

"Figure it out. You don't have much time."

"My head hurts. I need a few minutes. Just a few minutes rest."

I closed my eyes.

***

It was dark again. No, not totally dark, but the sun must have been setting. There was no more time, I needed to find a way out before the temperature dropped further.

I leaned backwards against the wall and tucked my legs underneath me. My thighs and calves burned with the effort but I stood. The wall was the only thing that kept me from falling as the vertigo returned.

The door was on the opposite wall from where I was standing. I needed to cross the room. I took one tentative step forward and the room spun. I retreated back to the wall.

"Okay, I'll just take the long way around." I moved sideways, bracing myself against the walls. There was a bench built into one side. I wanted to sit down on it, but I didn't dare. I might fall asleep again and lose even more time.

I admitted to myself that despite my earlier conclusion, the killer probably would come back eventually, if just to dispose of my body. Jake couldn't give him what he wanted, because he didn't know what it was. And even if he did know, once he gave it to the killer, I became a loose end that the killer would need to tie off.

The door had a slide bolt, the kind you see in public restrooms in individual stalls. But unlike those doors, there was something on the outside of this one, locking me in. Standing there, with fresh air coming in around the door, for the first time I could smell something other than my fear and the stale vomit in the room, I could smell the ocean. The roaring that I thought was all in my head, was due to the waves hitting the rocks. I was on the beach, in an old changing house.

My situation hadn't changed, but just knowing that much was a relief. I felt a little less lost.

Great, now use that information, Val. You won't be able to get out unless you get your hands free.

That little voice in my head was right. My hands were tied with multiple layers of duct tape, the dampness of the air, having loosened the tape only a fraction in the hours I'd been locked up.

I needed to find something to cut it.

The room was empty. No furniture. No objects on the floor. I stared at the walls. It was almost too dark now, but I saw a single exposed nail. Swimmers had probably hung their clothes on it while at the beach. I inched my way across and frantically scraped the duct tape against it.

"Ouch." In my eagerness to get my hands free, I managed to slice my palm on the rusty nail. It was a deep cut.

When did I last have a tetanus shot? Of course it wouldn't matter if the killer returned.

Blood trickled down my arm as I continued to rub my duct taped wrists against the nail. Finally, the small rip in the tape grew large enough for me to snap it and set my hands free.

Next step, getting out of the cell.

I felt like I was racing a lit fuse, but without a clear idea of when the bomb would go off, when the killer would return.

The shadows had grown darker during my struggle with the duct tape, but I thought I saw a hole in the floor.

The floor near the one wall I hadn't hugged on the trip to the door.

The wall on the ocean side.

The floor boards were rotten.

I leaned over carefully, nausea still a major concern, and felt the floor. It wasn't just a shadow. There was a small hole.

If I could make it bigger, I could get out. Since it was a bathhouse, it was elevated above the beach.

***

Kicking the floor in had been the easy part of the ordeal. Thank God no one had spent any money maintaining the historic structure. Underneath the bathhouse, I crawled through the drifted snow and sand and emerged on a rocky beach. I knew the recreational areas around Seamont. I'd never visited the ones in the neighboring communities. I scrambled up to the road, picked a direction, and walked.

I walked for what seemed like miles before I saw the lights of a gas station.

From the frightened expression on the teenager's face when I interrupted his marijuana break, I must have been quite a sight. The attendant was more than happy to give me an Orange Crush and let me call Jake instead of the police.

"Please, please have put the battery back in your cell phone," I prayed.

He picked up on the first ring.

"It's me." My throat was raw and I could barely get out any words.

"Where are you?" I held the phone away from my ear. I could hear the panic in Jake's voice.

I had no idea.

I looked at the teen. "What's this address?"

I was stunned to learn that we were in City Island, a tiny enclave on Long Island Sound, part of the Bronx, but adjacent to Westchester County.

I couldn't process the directions the teen was giving me. Wordlessly I handed the phone to the kid and sank to the floor. I scooted behind the desk, suddenly terrified that whoever had kidnapped me would return. I heard the kid give Jake directions and saw him nodding at whatever my husband was telling him.

I wrapped my arms around myself, trying to get warm, trying to stop shivering, although it wasn't the cold that was making me shake.

The teen kneeled next to me. "You sure you don't want me to call the police? Your husband's on his way. He's not the one who...."

I shook my head. It hurt. I wasn't going to do that again anytime soon. "I'm fine. My husband will know what to do."

This kid, undoubtedly losing any buzz he had, was nervous. He kept checking out the window.

Suddenly he announced, "Might be a good time to close early." He turned off the outer lights and left only a small light on in the office.

"Thanks." I could barely recognize my voice, shaky and raw.

As he locked up, I used the ladies room. Looking in the mirror, I hardly recognized myself. Half my face was bruised, the rest scratched. There was blood from the cut on my hand. I had two black eyes. I also had a dirty bandana looped around my neck, the cloth the kidnapper had blindfolded me with.

I put both hands on it and closed my eyes.

Nothing. I had no visions of anyone or anything. I just sensed fear and loathing. But it wasn't the terror of my kidnapper. It was my own.

***

"I'm sorry, lady. Your husband didn't come and you didn't come out of the bathroom. I waited a long time. I had to call the police."

I couldn't remember his name. Maybe I didn't know it. I couldn't focus properly but the face hovering over me looked like the teen from the gas station.

"Where's Jake?"

His face disappeared and I could hear him talking to someone else.

Had my kidnapper found me? I needed to leave.

I blinked a few times, trying to clear my vision. "What time is it?"

The face that came into view wasn't the gas station attendant's. It was a woman's face.

"I'm a paramedic. You're going to feel a slight prick. Just going to start an IV You've got a head injury but we're going to take good care of you. Do you know your name?"

I hesitated, there was a reason why I shouldn't tell them who I was. I just couldn't remember at the moment. "Valentine Zalmanzig."

There was some murmuring. A second voice talking to the one who had asked me my name.

"What did she say?"

"Valerie Zelman, I think. The stoner said she didn't have any identification on her."

"Good enough for now. Buckle that strap and she's ready to travel. Tell the cops to bring our Good Samaritan. The ER docs may want to ask him some questions."

***

There was a light shining in my eyes. It was making me feel nauseous again.

"Too bright," I mumbled, keeping my eyes shut. My voice sounded hoarse, scratchy.

A new voice spoke to me. An older man's voice. "Miss Zelman, who can we call for you? Can you give me the name of your next of kin?"

"Water? Can I have some water?"

"Just ice chips, we might have to operate, relieve some of the pressure that's building up in your head. Do you remember what happened?"

Operate? No. I wanted Jake. Where was he?

"Miss Zelman? Stay with me. What happened to you? Who hurt you?"

"Jake. Jake." I didn't understand why they wouldn't get him for me.

"What's Jake's last name?"

The man was asking me something. Maybe he would get Jake for me. "Cohen. Seamont."

I couldn't find the right words. Talking hurt my throat. I swallowed the ice chips and tried to think.

The man was talking again. "Someone tried to kill you? Who?"

Good questions, but I didn't have any answers.

***

The light was gone and I was cold. Too cold. My head ached. Something was pressing on my chest. Was I still in the bathhouse? Had I only dreamed that I'd escaped?

"Too cold. I can't stay here."

I tried moving my hands but they were still tied. My kidnapper could come back any time. I had to get out.

I could hear people talking above me, about me.

"Is it the fever or the concussion?"

"Hoping it's just the fever. Surgeon thinks the bleeding has stopped. He wants to wait and watch. We still don't have a medical history on her. Run another liter, let's get her hydrated."

"The guy who came in with her can't help?"

"He says he doesn't know her. She wandered into the gas station, beat up and confused."

"What about the police?"

"Talked to them. No one has reported a Valerie Zelman missing. They're looking for that Jake Cohen in Seamont that she mentioned. Will come here once they've got him."

The darkness was closing in on me again. But it was okay. Jake was on his way.

***

I kept trying to swim to the surface. I could hear sounds, but they seemed muffled, like I was underwater. I couldn't answer.

I groaned. Someone had grabbed my hand.

"That's a nasty wound. Deep."

Someone poured something cold on the hand and it stung badly. I tried to pull my hand away, but somebody held it in place, then tied my arm to a stiff board.

I struggled to sit up and get free. The kidnapper must have come back. He wasn't going to let me go unless Jake gave him what he wanted.

"Let me go. No. Jake. No."

I pulled at my arm and something came out.

I could hear shouting. "She pulled out the...."

I tried to stand up. I had to get out of there before the kidnapper and whoever was helping him killed me.

"Restraints. Put her in restraints. I'm going to stitch the hand."

They were tying me down. I was going to die.

"Jake, stop it." Where was Jake? Why wasn't he stopping the killer from hurting me?

I fought to get loose, but suddenly I felt a pinch in my arm and I slumped back down.

This time there was no sound, there was no light. Maybe this was death.

CHAPTER 21

"Valerie, time to wake up." It was a woman's voice.

Who was Valerie?

Someone patted my face. I flinched. The next touch wouldn't be soft.

"Can you open your eyes? I need you to open your eyes. Then you can sleep again."

She patted my face again, but again with a soft touch.

"Open your eyes Valerie. You're safe."

I opened them slowly. I had no idea where I was. Light was streaming into the room. I didn't recognize anyone. I tried to move, but my hands were tied to the bed rails.

I panicked. I started to struggle. "Don't hurt me."

My voice was thin and reedy, barely above a whisper.

A woman, in green surgical scrubs, leaned close and put a cool hand on my face. "I'm Dr. Moriah. You're in Montefiore Hospital. If you promise to leave the IV in place, we can remove the restraints. Do you understand?"

My heart was racing. Could I trust this woman? Where was Jake?

"Jake?"

The doctor gave a small smile. "He won't hurt you again. I promise."

I nodded. Maybe they had caught the kidnapper.

A nurse untied the restraints.

"Valerie, I need to examine you." She flashed a small penlight into each eye.

She asked me a series of questions about what year it was, the name of the President of the United States, my mother's name."

My head was still foggy, but I gave one word answers to each question, if slowly.

"On a scale of one to ten, what's the pain like in your head?"

I grimaced. "11. Lights…Nauseous."

I closed my eyes.

"That's okay, you can keep your eyes closed, but I want to tell you what we're doing to get you well."

I nodded for her to continue. It hurt to move my head. I remembered I'd decided not to do that anymore.

"You've got a Grade III concussion, worst you can get. You've got cuts, abrasions, and a very nasty wound on your hand, which we've cleaned and stitched. We gave you a tetanus shot. You're running a fever, probably from an infection. The lab is testing a blood sample to determine if it's bacterial or staph. In the meantime, we're giving you a broad range antibiotic in your IV. I also put in a sedative. You need to rest so your brain can repair itself. Concussions take time to heal."

I was so sleepy, but I opened my eyes. I squinted against the brightness of the overhead light. "Jake?"

The doctor smiled. "He's in jail. He won't hurt you again."

I fought to keep my eyes open. Why was Jake in jail? I wanted to tell them that Jake wouldn't hurt me. Why couldn't I find the words I needed?

She must have sensed my frustration. "You can't think of words, can you?"

I nodded frantically. It felt like a bomb went off in my head.

"Aphasia, the ability to express yourself, is sometimes one of the effects of a concussion. It will pass. You just need to rest."

I couldn't fight it anymore. The darkness took over again.

***

There were voices pulling me towards the surface. Strange voices. Men.

"I don't know why you got to be the lion."

"You're too short to be the lion. Perfect size for the scarecrow."

"One inch. One inch shorter than you."

"Might as well be a mile. You remember what mother always said."

"One of us got the looks, one of us got the brains."

"She never said which of us got what."

"You got the invitation?"

"Of course. We're due on the children's ward in 10 minutes. They don't need to know we took a brief stop in a client's room."

"She's not our client. Her husband is."

"I think she's waking up."

"Valentine, are you awake? I have a message from Jake. He wanted you to know he tried to find you, but the traffic was backed up on 95. By the time he got to the gas station to pick you up, it was closed and the ambulance was gone. The hospital screwed up your name and he couldn't find you. "

I tried to open my eyes, the lids were so heavy. "Jake? Need Jake."

"Valentine, you have to tell the doctors that Jake didn't hurt you. I've arranged for bail, but you have to tell them he wasn't the one who attacked you. Otherwise he can't come see you."

The second voice chimed in again and had an argument with the first.

"You just went to court and talked to the judge. I actually put up the money. Tell her that. You always claim all the glory."

"Don't be difficult. And lower your voice. Even with an invitation, they'll throw us out if we're caught in here."

I could hear them walking around my room. Who were they? Maybe the kidnapper sent them to make sure I didn't identify him. I needed to get some help.

"Hey, what's her file say?"

"Stable. Jake will be relieved. They're treating her for pneumonia and a nasty concussion."

"You realize that it was fate that her husband called us? It wasn't chance that Jake was in the same cell as Louis."

"It actually might have been a set up by the FBI. What are the odds that Louis would have our business card on him? The old drunk seldom even carries a wallet."

"Don't start with your conspiracy theories. Her name is Valentine. Our business is Heart Bail Bonds. Even you have to admit that's a sign. Powers beyond our control have set this in motion."

"And Assorted Legal Services. Heart Bail Bonds and Assorted Legal Services. Why do you always leave off that part?"

I groaned and fumbled for the call button. Nothing made sense. Where was Jake?

"Stop her. Don't let her–"

"Valentine? You have to tell them that Jake didn't hurt you."

I finally got my eyes open and saw a lion and scarecrow

"Is she awake?"

"Not sure. They're giving her some heavy duty drugs."

"Where's Jake?" I whispered.

The lion came closer. "Valentine, listen to me. Jake's bail was conditioned on him not coming within a mile of this hospital. He sent us."

"Did he send Toto too?"

I remembered Jake wanted a dog. I blinked and the lion came into focus and then it was dark again. The last words I heard were, "We'll be back tomorrow."

**

I was dreaming. It was one of those dreams where you knew you were dreaming but couldn't wake yourself up.

A small dog was walking in front of me. I was lost and I kept following the dog, hoping he would lead me home.

I was barefoot. And cold. And suddenly a shimmering ball drifted down in front of me and out stepped a beautiful woman in a ball gown with a tiara on her head and a wand in her hand.

"Can you help me?" I begged. Maybe she had the magic to end this nightmare.

'You don't need to be helped any longer. You've always had the power to go back to Kansas."

"Kansas?" Was she crazy? I didn't want to go to Kansas. Oklahoma maybe, but not Kansas.

She kept talking. "Close your eyes and tap your heels together three times. And think to yourself, 'there's no place like home'."

I looked down at my feet. "I don't have the ruby slippers. I don't know where to find them."

The witch frowned. "Sure you do. You just don't know you know."

I was so tired. "What does that mean? I don't know what I know. If I did, I'd tell you."

She tapped my nose lightly. "Look around. It's as plain as the nose on your face."

She faded away, but instead of darkness, there was light, very bright light.

I opened my eyes. A woman in a nurse's uniform was taking my blood pressure.

She smiled. "Finally awake. I'll get the doctor. She's making rounds on the ward."

She left the room and I was confused as ever.

I wasn't in Oz, I wasn't in Kansas.

***

A woman in her 40s, wearing a white lab coat with the name Dr. Moriah monogrammed on it, came into the room. Brisk, efficient, she immediately checked the chart hanging at the end of my bed.

"Your vitals are much stronger. Your temperature is way down. Sit up, lean forward, and let me listen to your chest."

The stethoscope was cold, as always. I coughed when asked, took deep breaths as instructed. She checked my eyes with her penlight.

She made a note on the chart. "Much better. How do you feel?"

I thought for a moment. "Confused."

She frowned. "Do you know your name?"

Was it Valerie Zelman? That didn't sound right. I had to think for a moment. "My name is Valentine Cohen."

I looked to see if I got it right. The doctor's face was impassive.

She asked me the year, who was President. I was nervous, but I knew the answers.

She nodded, then asked, "Do you know why you are here?"

"I was...Somebody hurt me." Images flashed in my mind and I began to shiver.

"Do you know who hurt you?"

I shook my head. "I couldn't see. He blindfolded me, tied my hands, and taped my mouth. I escaped."

The doctor pushed on. "Did you recognize his voice?"

I tried to remember. There was something vaguely familiar, but nothing I could identify. "I don't think so."

"Are you sure? Is it possible that it's someone you know? You don't have to be afraid. You're safe here. He can't get to you here."

I looked at the doctor. I felt like she knew something I didn't. "Who? You already know who did this to me?"

The doctor stood up. "When the paramedics brought you in, you identified your attacker. He's been arrested and can't come within one mile of you or risk revocation of his bail."

What a relief. Now maybe Jake and I could get back to our lives. "What's his name? Who did this to me? And why?"

The doctor looked confused. "You don't remember?"

"No. Who did I say? Have I lost my memory about the attack? Is it permanent?" I was getting scared. And where was Jake? Why wasn't he here with me? I wouldn't have left his side if he'd been hurt. Where the hell was my husband?

I could hear the beeping of the heart monitor begin to race.

The doctor put her hand on my shoulder. "You need to calm down. Memory loss is usually temporary. Given the severity of your concussion, it may take a few days, but you should recover completely."

I shook off her hand. "I'll calm down when you tell me who did this to me. No, forget that. You need to call my husband. I need to see Jake. Why isn't he here?"

Suddenly it struck me. Nothing would keep Jake from me unless...."Oh my God. Jake. He's dead, isn't he? Tell me the truth. The kidnapper killed Jake."

I started to sob.

"Mrs. Cohen, stop. Your husband isn't dead."

"I don't believe you. Nothing would keep Jake away from me. Where is he? Does the kidnapper have him? Please, what happened to my husband?"

The doctor sighed. "Mrs. Cohen, your husband has been arrested."

I was confused again. "For what?"

The doctor stood up. She murmured something to the nurse, who immediately left the room. "Jacob Cohen was arrested yesterday for the attempted murder of you."

"No, that's crazy," I shouted, my head beginning to pound. "Jake didn't hurt me. He'd never hurt me."

The nurse came back into the room with a syringe.

The doctor put something into my IV. "This is a sedative. I want you to rest. When you wake up, you can talk to the police and clear it all up."

And then there was darkness.

CHAPTER 22

I could hear a knocking, then voices, but they were muffled. I rose from the depths of the bottom of the bottomless pit and swam to the surface. I passed the Lion, the Scarecrow, and Toto on my way to–I didn't know where. At last I opened my eyes. Two men were at the doorway to my room.

I thought I recognized their voices, but I'd never met them before.

"Mrs. Cohen, may we come in?"

The men looked identical, although one was slightly taller than the other.

I nodded. I scooted up in the bed. "Do I know you?"

The taller one smiled. He was about 45, long straggly brown hair, pulled back in a messy ponytail at the nape of his neck. He wore a worn grey suit, wrinkled white shirt, and a tie of indeterminate color, but I was pretty sure those were pizza stains on it.

"My name is Michael Heart. I'm a lawyer representing your husband, Jacob Cohen."

The shorter one, whose short wiry hair framed a face almost identical to the man I assumed was his brother, pushed himself forward. He wore a pair of khaki slacks, a navy windbreaker, and his tie too sported his lunch.

"I'm Harold Heart, the bail bondsman who supplied the money for your husband's release. You can call me Harry."

I blinked and tried to remember. It was their voices. Suddenly it struck me. "You're the Lion and Scarecrow."

"Yes, ma'am," Michael Heart smiled. "Our mother is head of the volunteer group at the hospital. She roped us in to putting on a weekly show for the kids who are patients. We tell a story, sing a couple of songs." He shrugged, "This week was *The Wizard of Oz.*"

Maybe I wasn't losing my mind. It wasn't a dream, or at least not all of it. But as my head cleared, I focused on what brought them here. I tried to get out of bed, but was dizzy and nauseous. I fell back against the pillows.

"Wait, wait. You're not supposed to get excited. Our mother will kill us if we upset you," Harry Heart warned.

I grabbed Michael's hand. "The doctor said that Jake had been arrested for trying to kill me. You've got to get him out of jail. He didn't do it."

Harry pushed Michael out of the way again. "Don't worry Mrs. Cohen, your husband is out of the slammer. Made bail last night."

"Where is he? I think one of you told me that he couldn't come here. I think that's what the doctor said too."

Michael nodded. "It was one of the conditions for bail. He's at your home, but will have to move elsewhere once you are released from the hospital. He isn't allowed to call or visit. That's why I'm here." He pointed a thumb at his brother. "No good reason why he's here too. All he did was post bail. I'm your husband's lawyer."

I started to cry. "But Jake is innocent. What do I have to do to convince the judge to drop the charges? It's all just a horrible misunderstanding."

Michael patted my hand awkwardly, while Harry offered some tissues.

"Sorry. It all is just too much." I wiped my eyes and blew my nose. I was getting tired again and I hadn't done anything.

Michael pulled up a chair next to the bed. "Here's what I think is happening. The cops want to nail Jake for the murders of Lois and George Berman, as well as Margo

Cager. Arresting him for the attempted murder of you is just an excuse and buys them time to build their case for the other crimes."

It made sense. "But he didn't do any of those things. Do they have any evidence that links Jake to anything including kidnapping me?"

Michael shrugged. "You know the old expression that a DA can get a grand jury to indict a ham sandwich?"

I nodded.

"Jake's the ham sandwich."

I took a deep breath. "Can I take a lie detector test or something to at least clear Jake of hurting me?"

Michael smiled a crooked smile. "I don't think that will be necessary. Of course, I'll arrange for the police to interview you, but only about your abduction. I don't want you talking about the other murders. They'll use anything you say, even innocently, to build their case against Jake. The problem is that they'll see you as a victim of domestic violence who is afraid to tell the truth."

"So what can we do?"

Harry, who'd been leaning against the wall, stepped forward. "Your best hope is to find the real killer because the fuzz aren't looking for him. They've got a guy they like for it and they're going to make their case, with or without you."

"Just like they did with Alex Fletcher," I said.

Michael stood up and reached into his pocket. He handed me a man's antique pocket watch. I recognized it. I'd given it to Jake as a wedding present.

"He's not allowed to write to you so he asked me to give you this and tell you that he loves you. He said, and I hope I got this part right because it sounds sort of strange, but he says that the watch will keep you connected to him. Does that make sense?"

I smiled and closed my fingers around the gold case.

Michael walked to the door. "I've got an appointment with the detective in charge of the case, Diane something."

"Ellison, her name is Diane Ellison."

Michael nodded. "I'll talk to her and arrange for her to meet with you. Probably tomorrow afternoon."

"Okay." I could barely keep my eyes open.

I heard Harry as he walked out of the room. "You take care of yourself, Mrs. Cohen. You can count on us."

"We should get her some security." I think the voice was Michael's, the attorney.

Harry answered him. "I've got one of my contractors coming. I'll stay here until he arrives."

I clutched Jake's watch next to my heart. I thought for sure that I'd feel his comforting presence. But there was nothing, no psychic connection. Still I fell asleep to the steady tick of a gift of a better time.

***

"Valentine, how are you?"

I was sitting in a wheelchair in my room, the television mounted on the wall, flickering. The sound was muted. The nurse had given me the remote before rushing off to answer a page. I couldn't summon the energy to even turn up the sound.

If I'd been given a choice, I'd have stayed in bed. But I wasn't asked and my protests were ignored. The hospital ran on a schedule and it didn't matter what I wanted. Of course that's not what I was told. The nurses assured me that a shower and breakfast would make me feel like a new woman. So far all I'd felt was exhausted and increasingly angry at my situation.

Seeing Detective Ellison walk into my room with a small fruit basket didn't improve my attitude. Apparently she decided to come five hours early in order to meet without my lawyer present.

"How are you feeling, Valentine?"

"I'm sure you don't care about my health, Diane. I'm also sure you are well aware that Jake would never hurt me. So don't bother with the pleasantries, just tell me what you really want."

The detective's smile disappeared, replaced by a look of consternation. I reminded myself that the woman had fooled me more than once and that I had keep my guard up.

Diane crossed the room and set the basket of oranges and grapes on the window sill. I had the sense she was stalling for time, trying to gauge what approach might work best with me.

"Val, please. I care. I'm so sorry you believe otherwise." She leaned against the end of my bed and pleaded her case. "You misunderstand my motives. I'm just doing my job, trying to find the person who killed the Bermans and your friend Margo. I don't wish either you or Jake harm. But I can't ignore the evidence either."

Remembering Michael Heart's admonition not to discuss the murders with the police, I remained silent.

"I don't think you know your husband as well as you think you do. Perhaps you're too close to see what I see. The connection between the Changs, the Bermans, Margo, and even Stan Freedman is Jake. He doesn't have an alibi for any of the murders."

I opened my mouth to dispute that, then realized she had to be baiting me, trying to get me to talk.

"Jake didn't kill anyone, you'll never make me believe otherwise."

"It's hard. I get it. He played you from the very beginning. I talked to people who attended Alex Fletcher's murder trial. They said Jake sat in the audience every day. That's where you two met, right? He found some pretext to approach you? Find out what you knew about the Chang murders? You were something he didn't plan for, something unpredictable. I imagine he was scared when he realized that the police were using a psychic to check out potential suspects."

My headache was back. I knew she was wrong, but would a jury? The police could force a square peg into a round hole if they kept twisting the facts to suit their theories. If she wanted to scare me, she was doing a good job.

I cleared my throat. "I think you should leave and come back when my attorney is here."

"You mean Michael Heart? He's your husband's attorney? Although using the word attorney in relation to the man is a stretch. The man believes the government is hiding aliens in Roswell, New Mexico. There isn't a conspiracy theory that Michael Heart doesn't embrace. And his brother is even stranger. He practices bending spoons. Val, I strongly advise you to get an attorney of your own. Someone who represents you and–"

"Just stop!" I couldn't listen to her any more. "Diane, you are wasting time. The real killer is still out there and he's not done, not by a long shot. He's looking for something. Something he–"

I started coughing. My chest felt tight.

Diane glanced around and found the water jug on the bedside table. She poured me a cupful. "I don't mean to upset you. But you need to listen to me. We have evidence against Jake. This is real, Val. I'm not making this up."

I drank the water and then managed to croak out the question Diane wanted me to ask. "What evidence?"

"Yes, what evidence?" An irritated Michael Heart took center stage as he stalked into the room. Righteous indignation rolled off him in waves. "Do tell us, detective."

"Okay. Fine." Diane shrugged. "I'll tell you. We went back to the Berman house. A few days after we had you walk through it. We searched it again and we found some prints we didn't find the first time. We found your husband's prints. Jake Cohen was in that house, in the master bedroom. His prints were on the bedpost. There is no innocent explanation for that."

I started coughing again and Michael stepped out to find a nurse. Diane waited, her expression one of pity.

Damn. There was an explanation, but I couldn't tell her. This was my fault. I'd talked Jake into going with me, talked him into visiting with the victims.

A nurse came bustling in, irritated with everyone, including me. "All of you need to get out. I can't have the patient getting upset."

I held up my hand and pointed to Michael. "He's my lawyer. Just a few more minutes."

"Two minutes. I don't have time for this nonsense. You,"–the nurse pointed to Diane–"Need to leave right now."

Diane nodded and picked up her coat. "Val, believe it or not, I'm trying to protect you."

"Detective Ellison," Michael said firmly. "I'm filing a notarized statement from Val with the court swearing that her husband did not assault her. At a minimum, I want the bail conditions altered to allow Val and Jake to be together."

"And when he kills her?"

I struggled to stand, clutching the tray table for support. "Get out."

The room started to spin. Michael caught me and eased me back into bed.

The nurse came in. "That's it. All of you get out or I'm calling security."

Diane left immediately. The nurse stood glaring at Michael.

"Val, get some rest. I'll come back this afternoon with the secretary from my office and a notary. I'll file the paperwork with the court either late this afternoon or first thing in the morning."

I struggled for breath. "Will they let me go home with Jake? The doctor said I would probably be discharged tomorrow."

Michael shrugged. "Don't know. Might give me a quick ruling; DA might fight me. Jake has agreed to stay at the Residence Inn in New Rochelle so you can be in the house."

I shook my head. "I want...."

Michael squeezed my hand. "I know what you want. I also know that Jake wants you safe. We've got some plans in place in case the court doesn't grant a change in the bail conditions."

"What plans?"

The nurse tapped on her watch. "Now, mister."

Michael slipped on his coat. "Let's take this step-by-step."

The nurse took my pulse, made a note on my chart, and left.

I didn't think I'd sleep. My mind was racing as fast as my heart. But I was wrong.

***

I had the same dream again. Glinda, the good witch, came floating down in the bubble.

Once again, I told her, "I want to go home."

Glinda told me that I already knew how to get to Kansas. "The answer is as plain as the nose on your face."

I woke up angry and frustrated. I lay in bed, trying to figure it all out. Did something happen in Kansas that was connected to all of this? What was it about my nose? What did I know that I didn't realize I knew? I'd only succeeded in working myself up to another coughing fit, and another stern lecture from the nurse. I wondered when her shift would be over. She was wearing me out.

"I come bearing gifts."

Harry Heart stood in the doorway, with a small suitcase and a bag from Stew's, my favorite luncheonette.

"Jake wasn't sure when you would be released, but he packed a bag of clothes, cosmetics, stuff like that. He also was sure that the food was terrible and thought you'd like some of Stew's chicken soup and a liverwurst sandwich. I asked if he was kidding about the liverwurst, but he assured me that he wasn't. Really, you like liverwurst?"

I grinned. First time I think I'd smiled in days. "Gimme."

I tore open the bag and inhaled the smells. "My Grandmother loved the stuff. The two of us were the only ones in the family who did. As Gran would say when everyone else would turn up their noses, 'More for us'."

Suddenly I thought about my family. "My mother! She must be scared out of her mind."

Harry shook his head. "Jake said to tell you that he told your mother that you were on a buying trip and would call when you got back. She's called a half-dozen times, so I'm not sure she believed him. He said maybe you should give her a call as soon as you can."

I fell back against the pillows. "Thank God. If she knew she'd be on the first plane here, along with my aunt. I love them to bits, but that's the last thing I need right now."

I started to eat, but good manners took over. "You want half?"

Harry shook his head vehemently. "I'm with the rest of your family. Ugh. Okay, if I sit here with you? I'm a notary and will affix my seal to your affidavit."

I took a spoonful of the soup. It was delicious and felt wonderful on my throat. I alternated between the soup and the sandwich, and had almost finished both when Michael arrived with an older woman who he introduced as Rita, his secretary. She unpacked her briefcase and set up her laptop computer and travel printer on the tray table next to the bed.

"Are you feeling well enough to go over what happened to you?" Michael asked.

I nodded. "Give me a second to see if I can get it in order. It's still kind of a blur."

"Take your time."

I told my story, stopping occasionally to get myself under control. I felt panicky when I recounted the blindfold, the tape across my mouth, the kidnapper's vicious slaps because I didn't give him the answer he wanted.

Michael was quiet until I finished, then asked, "Did you recognize your attacker?"

"No. At one point I thought his voice was familiar, but now I think that he was disguising it."

"What do you mean?"

I thought for a moment. "It sounded like the Jolly Green Giant commercials I used to see on television when I was growing up. Sort of like "Ho, Ho, Ho, Green Giant." I tried to make my voice sound deep like the cartoon character who hawked frozen vegetables.

"How do you know that it wasn't your husband disguising his voice?"

I closed my eyes and went back to the car ride. "It was a stick shift. We don't own a stick shift car. I could hear him shifting gears."

I opened my eyes and smiled triumphantly.

Michael nodded, but pressed me. "Suppose your husband had a car hidden that had a stick shift. Or maybe it was a rental."

I blew out a breath. "Give me a break, that's ridiculous."

"Think, Val. Is there anything else you can remember that told you it wasn't Jake Cohen who abducted you?"

I closed my eyes again. This time, I focused on the place he'd taken me to and then I knew. "He's taller than Jake. A good three or four inches taller. When he forced me to walk to the bath house, I was leaning against him. My head barely came up to his shoulder."

My eyes flew open. "It can't be Jake. The kidnapper was taller."

Michael, Harry, even Rita smiled.

The next few minutes were spent while I reviewed and signed the affidavit. Harry then notarized it. Rita and Harry left, headed to the courthouse. She said she hoped to file the paperwork before the clerk left for the day; Harry said he'd gotten a call from someone just arrested looking to make bail.

I was physically exhausted and emotionally spent. "So will this clear Jake?"

Michael sighed. "It should. But Jake's still a person of interest for the other murders. The DA and cops are going to try and enforce the conditions of bail just to harass him a little. They'll say you are lying to protect him. We'll probably win, but it may take a day or two."

"So I still can't talk to him?"

Michael patted me on the shoulder. "Patience, Val. The wheels of justice move slowly, but sure."

It was of little comfort.

After Michael left, I started to clean up the remains of my lunch. There was something left in the Stew's bag. It was a black and white cookie, a New York deli specialty, and my favorite. I looked closely and saw something written on the plastic wrap.

"Forever. Jake."

CHAPTER 23

It was actually two days before I could go home. I was running a small fever and my doctor refused to discharge me until my temperature was normal. Personally I think the fact I had good health insurance played a major role in the hospital wanting to extend my stay, but what do I know.

Everything at the house looked the same, but it didn't feel the same. I'd been ignoring a nagging feeling that had developed over the last couple of days that something more than the concussion and the pneumonia was wrong with me. Walking into the home that I'd shared for almost five years with Jake and his family, the truth hit me like a slap on the face. No disembodied voices. No visions. When I touched an object I didn't experience the thoughts or emotions of another person. I felt alone. For the first time in my life, I knew that the only person in my head was me.

"Which way is your kitchen? And why is your door unlocked?" Harry Heart walked into my living room with his arms full of grocery bags.

Michael Heart had warned me when he dropped me off that his brother was coming to stay with me until Jake got home. I wasn't crazy about it, but Michael said it would only be for a few hours. There was a hearing in front of the judge that afternoon. Michael was confident that Jake would be able to move back home afterwards.

"I'll show you. Watch out for the boxes. We were having a new furnace put in before this...this thing happened."

"Yeah, Jake told me. Word on the street is that Richard Baez is in the wind. But he'll show up again, looking for money from his daddy. I got a guy watching the old man."

I helped Harry unpack the bags. I had to hide a smile at what I discovered. The choices had teenage boy written all over them. Harry had chosen an amazing assortment of frozen food: pizzas, eggrolls, mini-hamburgers, burritos, and chicken wings. He'd also thrown in a gallon of milk, a carton of eggs, two loaves of bread, sandwich meat, processed cheese slices, peanut butter, chips, pretzels, beer and ice cream bars. There wasn't a green, leafy item to be seen.

"I never realized that a bail bondsman offered this kind of service," I joked, wondering again how my conservative Jake had chosen to rely on the unusual, okay maybe peculiar, brothers.

Harry grinned and pulled two beers back out of the refrigerator, offering me one. I begged off, making noises about not mixing alcohol with my medication. He nodded and put the second bottle in his jacket pocket for later.

"I recognized your name," Harry said. "When I got the call I remembered reading about you in the newspapers, back during the Fletcher murder trial. Seems to me the police used and abused you that time too. I tried calling you to offer Michael's services then, but your line was always busy. I guess you were getting a lot of crank calls after the word got out about your psychic talents."

Opening the bag of pretzels, I shook some out into a bowl. "You called me during the Fletcher trial? Why?"

"Thought you might need some protection. The world just doesn't appreciate sensitive types like us. Our powers threaten their world view."

I'd made the mistake of putting one of the pretzels in my mouth at the same time Harry referred to himself as sensitive. Choking it down, I barely avoided finding out if Harry had "first responder" skills in addition to his other...what did he say?

"Powers?" I finally asked when I caught my breath.

He nodded. "I'm psychic too," he confided in a whisper. "Not as good as you, but I'm very intuitive. Mostly I hone my skills at the track, but it comes in handy at work too. Like when Jake called and asked for help, I knew it was my destiny to assist you in your search."

"Search?" Why would Harry choose that word? Did he know what the killer was looking for? Maybe there was more than fate involved with the Heart brothers' invasion of our lives. Or maybe I was just catching Jake's paranoia.

"Search for the murderer," Harry said without hesitation. "Hey, do you want me to make you a sandwich? I didn't eat breakfast."

I wasn't hungry but I had an antibiotic to take and I'd been warned not to take it on an empty stomach. "Okay, thanks."

The sound of the front door slamming, ended the sandwich making discussion.

"That was quick," I exclaimed, heading for the foyer. I called back over my shoulder, "Must be Jake and your brother."

"Valentine wait. It can't be...."

The crying stopped us both in our tracks.

Harry pulled a handgun from his shoulder holster. I hadn't even realized he carried a gun. Jake and I were going to have to have a long talk about his new associates. His second cousin was looking better to me all the time.

Despite Harry's admonitions to stay back, I followed him to the front door.

I'd never seen the car seat sitting on my entrance hallway floor before, but I recognized the very angry baby screaming his head off.

***

A young woman scooped the frantic baby from his car seat. She slipped a pacifier in the infant's mouth and murmured soothing words. In a moment, he settled down, looking around the entry foyer with wide eyes.

"I'm Alisha Warren."

She said it matter-of-factly, like I would of course recognize the name.

I nodded. She looked to be about 30, short blonde hair, very thin.

"You're Valentine Cohen?" This time it was a question.

I nodded again. I was so stunned that I seemed to have lost my voice.

She continued. "And this is Jake Cohen? The man who rescued my baby?"

That was enough to shake me out of my reverie. "No. This is…"

How to describe who Harry was and why he was there? "No. Jake isn't here."

"Oh." She said it with such sadness that I had no idea what was going on.

My mother's instructions on hospitality kicked in. "Can I help you? Would you like a cup of tea?"

Actually my mother would have been appalled at the whole mess I was in and etiquette would have been the least of her worries.

"Yes, please."

I headed toward the kitchen, with mother, baby, and unofficial bodyguard in tow.

Harry had holstered his handgun and sat across from Alisha and her baby. I busied myself making a pot of English Breakfast tea, although I momentarily thought that brandy would be a better choice. I put out a plate of cookies as well.

The baby continued sucking vigorously on his pacifier while taking in his surroundings. Alisha didn't speak until I'd joined them at the table.

"When will Mr. Cohen be back?"

"I don't know. He's...." Again, I wasn't sure what, if anything, to say about Jake's current living situation.

Alisha took a sip of tea. "You look like," she paused. She clearly seemed to be choosing her words carefully, "Like you've been in an accident."

That brandy would definitely have been better than the tea. I decided to cut to the chase.

"Mrs. Warren, what do you want?"

My words were louder or harsher than I should have spoken, but I was physically tired and emotionally drained. She was just another stranger that had invaded my home and my life without invitation. They all seem to want something from me and I was in no mood to wait for her to get to the point of her visit.

The baby startled at my voice and began to fuss.

Alisha Warren looked around the room, then asked, "Do you have a dish towel I could borrow?"

Okay. A dish towel I could manage. I got a clean one from the drawer. She draped it over her shoulder, lifted her sweater, and put the baby to her breast. She discreetly covered her chest with the dishcloth.

Harry turned bright red and excused himself. "I'll be in the living room if you need me."

Her voice was so quiet I could barely hear her. "I have some antiques for sale."

I stood up. "I'm sorry. The business is closed." I didn't add, possibly for good, but that certainly was a likely outcome.

She grabbed my hand. "Please. They're really special. A good price. I'm sure Mr. Cohen would be interested."

I shook it off. "Mrs. Warren–"

I looked at the nursing infant and lowered my voice, "If you're here to sell antiques, you've come to the wrong place at a very bad time. I think you should go."

Her eyes filled with tears. "Please, I need money. I've got to get Christopher away from here. Take the antiques and just give me enough for a train ticket to Syracuse. My folks live there."

It was time to get some answers. "Where's your husband?"

She shook her head. The tears ran down her face and dripped onto the towel covering her nursing infant. "Dead. Murdered two nights ago. Dumped into the Sound. Christopher and me, we've been running ever since."

The words hit me with the force of hurricane winds. Another murder. I'd been lucky, I'd barely escaped the same fate as her husband. The room started to spin. I carefully gripped the table, fighting the bile rising in my throat.

"Mrs. Cohen, Mrs. Cohen?"

I could hear her cries, but couldn't answer. Harry ran into the room.

He angrily demanded to know what had happened.

The baby began to wail.

I sank to the floor, crawled over into a corner, shut my eyes tight, and covered my ears.

For a second I was back in that bathhouse, sure that any minute I was going to be killed.

I thought I could block it all out, will both Alisha Warren, Christopher, and even Harry away. I'd begun my counting routine to slow my breathing, when suddenly I heard someone else race into the room.

"What the hell is going on?"

I opened my eyes.

Jake was home at last.

CHAPTER 24

Harry frowned at Jake, who was walking around the living room holding the now calm baby. "Hey, man, you're not going to keep the little dude are you? Kids unbalance my chakra."

"Your what?" Jake came to a stop next to where I was reclining on the sofa.

"His bliss," I mumbled, adjusting the damp washcloth on my forehead and wondering if I'd gotten out of the hospital too soon. "Did someone say where Michael is?"

Harry set the platter of sandwiches on the coffee table, then answered her. "My brother will be here soon. He had a meeting with the detectives on the Berman murders. He's trying to understand why they are so convinced that Jake is involved."

"I'd like to know that too," Jake said as he handed the baby back to Alisha. "The whole time they were interrogating me I got the feeling they had some evidence they weren't sharing. Something that pointed to me. In case anyone has any doubts, I didn't kill anyone, but someone is going to a lot of trouble to make it look like I did."

"Valentine, you should sit up and eat so you can take your pills." Harry pushed a sandwich into Jake's hands. "Feed your wife and let Michael worry about keeping you out of jail."

"Mrs. Warren, you have a sandwich too. I'm going to get everyone a glass of milk." The bail bondsman left the room before anyone could object.

I could have used some coffee instead. Jake had been eyeing Harry's beer, so I know milk wasn't on his mind. Mrs. Warren appeared to just be waiting for another chance to talk business with Jake.

Groaning, I did as Harry demanded and sat up. Jake sat down next to me and held up a peanut butter sandwich to my mouth.

"I can feed myself, thank you."

Jake nodded and gave it to me. "Just trying to help."

Alisha cleared her throat. "Excuse me, I appreciate the food and the chance to catch my breath, but I'm kind of in a rush. I need to get out of town before the man who killed my husband finds me and Christopher."

There were questions that had to be asked and it appeared I was the only one who was willing to push the point. "Who killed your husband?"

Alisha shook her head. "I don't know."

"Where's his body? Did you call the police?"

Again, Alisha shook her head. "I can't call the cops. I've got to protect Christopher. It's what Rudy would want."

I slapped the sandwich back on the plate and stood up. The whole thing didn't make sense. I was angry that we were being sucked into this woman's drama. Jake just seemed ensorcelled by the baby. One of us had to think straight. I ticked off the questions on the fingers of my hand, my voice getting louder with each one.

"How do you know he's dead? How do you know the cops aren't going to find the body and come looking for you and Christopher? How do you know the killer, if there really is a killer, won't find you here? How do we know your husband isn't a killer?"

The questions were coming so fast that I could barely catch my breath. I started to cough and struggled to remain standing. I felt Jake's arms around me, as he forcibly settled me back on the couch. I shrugged off his embrace. I was angry with everyone and that included my husband.

The baby started to cry. Alisha walked around the living room, jiggling the infant, trying to get him to settle down.

As soon as Christopher had quieted, Jake said in much too calm a voice, "Why don't we all sit down and talk this through."

I was ready to kill him, but was focused on not coughing up a lung.

Alisha perched on the edge of a Windsor chair, holding and patting Christopher.

Harry came back to the living room, this time with a mug of hot tea instead of the threatened milk. My hands were shaking so hard that tea sloshed over the top.

"Val, calm down." Jake leaned forward. "Alisha, start at the beginning."

Her voice was so soft, I could barely hear her. I guess she was speaking quietly because she didn't want to wake Christopher whose eyes were at half-mast.

"You have to understand that money was tight and with the baby and trying to buy the building where our apartment is, we got in over our heads."

Jake nodded.

"So we got into the antiques business. Sometimes we purchased things at auction, and sometimes we...." She stumbled over her words, "Sometimes we acquired items in a less structured way."

"I see," Jake said. "Did you acquire any items from Lois and George Berman? Or maybe Margo Cager? Or Stan Freedman?"

Alisha shrugged. "We sold things to Stan on a regular basis. He won a lot of our eBay auctions." She glanced down at the sleeping Christopher.

"Did you acquire items from the Bermans or Margo Cager?"

She nodded. "We knew we'd made a mistake when Margo tracked us down. She was in a panic about something we'd–"

"Stolen?" I found my voice. "You stole from Margo?"

Alisha wouldn't meet my eyes, but she nodded. "Margo had security cameras and she recognized Rudy from the veterinary clinic. She said she wouldn't go to the police but we had to give her back the wooden silverware chest we'd taken. We would have, but we'd already–"

"You'd already resold it." Jake finished her sentence and added another question. "Who did you sell it to?"

Alisha hugged her baby a little tighter. "Stan Freedman. We tried to get it back but the old man wouldn't listen. Margo threatened us, she was behind the carjacking. We didn't know what to do. After we got Christopher back, we started staying with friends. Rudy quit his job at the clinic."

"What was in the silverware chest? Did Margo say why it was important?" Jake asked. He'd started pacing, leaving me alone on the sofa.

Harry sat in a wingback chair, eating sandwiches and chugging milk. He was dropping crumbs right and left on Jake's mother's favorite chair. Good thing she wasn't around to see it. His mother's current location was another thing I needed to discuss with Jake.

Alisha shook her head in response to Jake's question. "She just said she had to have it back. She sounded frightened when we finally admitted we didn't have it.

Please, Christopher and I need to get away from here. I've got some Revolutionary War-era silver salt cellars that Rudy thought were worth–"

Jake held up his hand. "We saw what you were storing in that bakery below your apartment. We don't handle novelty items or reproductions."

"We don't buy stolen merchandise either," I added. "We're in enough trouble as it is."

Alisha shook her head and Christopher shifted in his sleep. "No. All you saw was the junk we used to hide the real items when we shipped them. The salt cellars are the real deal."

She still hadn't answered the big question. I asked it again. "What about your husband? How do you know he's dead? Did you see his killer?"

Alisha started crying. "We've been moving from place to place. We slept in the car a couple of nights. Yesterday, Rudy left Christopher and me at the Mt. Vernon library. We used to go there all the time. I…I like to read. Rudy took the car, was going back to the apartment to pack up some clothes, toys, as much of our stuff as he could. He knew someone who could get us," her voice dropped to a whisper. "He knew someone who could get us fake identities. We were going to start over. The deal was after he got the paperwork, he'd come back and get me and the baby. Then we'd start driving to Syracuse. Rudy was going to leave me with my parents and look for work, maybe in Canada."

Alisha closed her eyes. Without opening them, she continued. "It was near to closing time. I couldn't call Rudy. We'd tossed our cell phones days ago. I didn't know what to do. One of the librarians let me use the staff room to nurse Christopher. There was a knock at the door. I thought they were going to kick me out so they could close up. One of the librarians I knew handed me an envelope. Said she'd found it at the reference desk."

Alisha opened her eyes and looked at me. I didn't want to know what was in the envelope. I didn't want to hear anymore. The pain in her eyes, the way she clutched Christopher, I knew she was telling the truth.

Jake kneeled in front of Alisha. "There's no question that he's dead?"

The young woman stifled a cry of despair. "It was a photo of Rudy with his throat slit. A second photo was of him sinking into water. There was a note in the envelope."

Jake nodded for her to continue. "What does the killer want?"

"He wants the last piece of the Pennsylvania map. I don't know what he's talking about. We never had any maps. I've got to get away. Please buy the salt cellars and–"

Jake clasped her hand. "We don't want the antiques, but we will buy you a train ticket to Syracuse. Let me check the schedule. The train leaves from Yonkers."

Alisha sat back in the chair. Christopher snuggled closer.

At last we had one answer to the puzzle. The killer wanted a piece of a map. The last piece of a map. A map of Pennsylvania? Was Pennsylvania a code word for something else? How many pieces where there? Did the killer have the other pieces? Why does he think we had one?

CHAPTER 25

It was the caped child dream. A boy, wearing a dishcloth cape, poised on the windowsill of my bedroom window. He's reaching out for something. The tree is too far away. It's too late.

"No," I screamed.

I woke up in a pool of sweat. Maybe I was still running a fever, despite the deluge of antibiotics coursing through my veins. More likely, it was the terrors I felt, awake and asleep.

I'd gone upstairs for a nap while Jake drove Alisha and baby Christopher to the train station. She had called her folks and they would be waiting for her in Syracuse. She gave us their number and we promised to keep her informed. We hadn't figured out what, if anything to tell the police.

Before she left, she begged me to try and keep her out of this mess. "I know I don't have a right, but please don't tell the cops about what Rudy and I were doing. We made a mistake, a big mistake, but Christopher–" She stifled a sob, "Christopher shouldn't have to pay for it. I'll go to prison and then who will take care of my baby?"

I had no idea if we could keep her out of it. Maybe the cops could find a clue from Rudy's body, but Alisha had no idea where the killer had dumped him. Eventually the body would probably wash ashore, but in the meantime, making sure mother and child were safe was the priority.

It was already dark outside. I glanced at the clock and couldn't believe that I'd slept for two hours. And yet I still felt so tired. Maybe I wouldn't feel rested again until this living nightmare was over. I walked out of my bedroom and heard voices from the living room below.

"She doesn't know?" It sounded like Michael Heart.

"Why is it important now?" It was Jake talking. His voice faded in and out so I suspected he was pacing, moving from the living room to the dining room and back again.

"Because if you could lie about that...."

I couldn't hear the rest of his sentence. I sat down on the top step and immediately got up again. My instinct was to go back to bed, pull the covers over my head, and hide from whatever bad news they were discussing. I stood there, frozen, when I heard Jake again. "She'll never forgive me."

As if in a trance, I walked down the stairs. The creak on the fifth step gave me away.

"Val, you okay?" Jake voice got stronger. He was in the dark entry foyer. I wished I could see his face, but it was shrouded in the shadows.

"I thought you might be down for the count. You need your rest." He was chattering, the nervous Jake making an appearance. "You want something to eat? Drink?"

I ignored his question and walked into the living room. Michael Heart was on the couch; Harry in the same wing chair where I'd left him hours earlier.

Michael started to rise, but I motioned to him to stay put. Instead he moved to the far end of the sofa. There was a bottle of Scotch on the coffee table. Michael and Harry's glasses seemed barely touched; Jake's was almost empty.

I looked at the three of them. When no one spoke, I asked, "What did the police say?"

Jake and Michael exchanged glances. Jake finished his Scotch.

I looked at my husband. "What is it? Tell me."

Jake kept his distance. He wouldn't meet my eyes. His voice was low and he spoke slowly, choosing each word carefully. "You have to understand, Val. I was in a bad place. I needed the money so I could keep this house, our house."

He waved his hand around.

I was lost. "What are you talking about?"

He started pacing again. I don't know who he was talking to, but it wasn't me. He seemed to be reciting a practiced speech. "I was three months behind on the mortgage payments, the shop was in the red. I was a historian who'd decided that going into antiques was a better way to make a living than teaching. I picked the wrong time, the economy was tanking when I made the switch. I'd already cashed in my 401K and was going to have to pay taxes on that…You have to understand Val. I was desperate and I regretted it almost immediately. But it was too late."

I stood up and grabbed his arm. "Tell me. What did you do? What do the police have on you?"

He wouldn't look at me. I turned his face toward mine. "Whatever it is, just say it."

He didn't answer.

I tried to think of what he could have done that was so bad. "Did you buy stolen merchandise? Fake the authenticity of items? For God's sake Jake, what the hell did you do?"

He closed his eyes, then opened them to stare at me for a few seconds, saying nothing. And then, ever so quietly, he said, "I sold you out for money. The Enquirer paid me $20,000 for my story, and I made it good." He stepped away from me. "You remember, don't you Val, how the news reports went. Valentine Zalmanzig, fake psychic, almost screwed up the case against the vicious killer who slaughtered a lovely couple in the nice All-American village of Seamont, New York. I got even more for the follow-up story that ran on Enquirer Tonight, the television show. I almost made it on Geraldo, but by then...."

He shook his head.

I was in a cold sweat by time he finished his confession. What else was there for him to say? I needed to know it all. "By then, what?"

Jake gave a small smile. "By then, I was falling in love with you."

I slapped him so hard that I could see my handprint on his cheek.

"Son of a bitch. Love me? You almost destroyed me." I screamed and slapped him again. Our whole life together had been a lie.

Jake didn't move, taking my verbal and physical assault, barely flinching. "I wanted to tell you, I swear."

"What else don't I know about you? Did you kill seven people so you could save your business? Was I next on your list?"

This time he did flinch. "Val, you don't believe that."

I swiped away the tears that were coursing down my face. "I don't know what I believe. You were right about one thing. I must be a fake psychic because I had no clue about you. I could have gone to my grave believing you loved me."

"Val," he stepped forward and I put up my hand to stop him.

"Don't, just don't."

I took a deep breath and turned to Michael. "Do the cops have anything else on Jake?"

Michael looked at Jake. What else had he done?

"They know?" Jake asked.

Michael nodded. "The ex-husband suspected. He told the police."

"But it was over years ago, before my marriage. Why does it matter now?"

I was more confused than ever. "Spit it out. What the hell else have you done?"

Jake took a deep breath and then said it so quickly, I almost missed it. I wished I had.

"Margo and I were lovers."

I thought I would throw up. "You cheated on me?"

"No, absolutely not."

I laughed. Like I could believe anything he said.

"Val, it was before we met."

"But while she was still married, right? No moral qualms about sleeping with a married woman. Morals are for other people, right? The stupid ones like me who actually believe in the sanctity of marriage, mine and other people's."

Jake sighed. "She wasn't happy in the marriage. I was having trouble with the store. My mother was sick. Margo's marriage fell apart long after we broke up."

"She was probably hoping that you'd be perfectly okay with continuing a little something on the side after we got married. Was that why she was here so much? Was that what made her such a good client?"

"Stop it Val. Margo and I were friends before we were lovers, and yes, we remained friends after you and I got together. You're still in touch with old boyfriends. The cops are just spinning this into something dirty. Believe it or not, Margo liked you. Thought we were right for each other."

I turned to Michael. "Anything else?" Not that I could take much more.

Michael shook his head. "Nothing besides the fingerprints in the Berman house and you know how they got there, and this. They assume that if he lied to you...."

He didn't finish the sentence.

And maybe they were right. What was Jake Cohen capable of doing? I wasn't sure anymore.

Jake spoke softly. "I'll go back to the Residence Inn. Harry will stay here to protect you. You're right to hate me, but Val, I didn't kill any of them. That much you have to know."

I thought for a moment and then asked, "If he moves out, will it convince the cops that I am afraid of Jake. That I believe he tried to kill me?"

"Doesn't matter," Jake interrupted.

I waved him off.

Michael shrugged. "It wouldn't help his case, that's for sure, but if you're more comfortable, that's what's important."

I said a silent prayer that I could see into the future, have a premonition, get some vibes that told me the right answer. But there was nothing. I'd have to go on my gut feeling, based on nothing but hope and almost five years of being married to this man, loving him with everything I had.

I made a decision. "Jake, you can stay here for now. Take a guest bedroom. There's plenty to choose from. We'll figure out whether there is any *us* later."

I was going back to bed and hoped to hell that I didn't dream.

CHAPTER 26

I didn't have to worry about dreaming. I didn't fall asleep until almost 5 in the morning. And then I slept the sleep of the dead. A bomb could have gone off next to me and I wouldn't have stirred. Which gave me pause when I finally did wake up. Would I know if anyone was trying to kill me in my sleep? Anyone like my husband?

Actually, after tossing and turning most of the night, I'd finally come to the conclusion that Jake wasn't the killer. It wasn't an emotional decision. Whoever had abducted and beaten me was part of this whole mess, and Jake wasn't that person. He wasn't the kidnapper. Of that I was sure.

But the angry feelings of betrayal flooded back like the winter sunlight pouring through the windows. This time, unlike the previous mornings since the kidnapping, I actually woke up feeling better, physically at least. A quick look in the mirror confirmed that the bruises were fading, nothing a good bottle of concealer couldn't hide. My chest didn't feel as tight. The antibiotics had finally kicked in.

My hand was still sore but the stitches would come out soon.

The big question was what to do about Jake? Not the long-term, "do I kick him to the curb once this was all over" dilemma, but the "what, if anything, do I say to him this morning" problem. Just how normal was I supposed to behave?

The rumbling noises from my stomach convinced me that I had to leave my bedroom and confront the issue sooner rather than later. My appetite had returned, which was another sign that I was on the road to recovery.

A quick shower, some well-worn jeans and a warm Irish fisherman's sweater, one of Jake's first gifts to me, and I headed downstairs.

The smell of coffee drew me to the kitchen, but the sight of Jake sitting at the kitchen table, hunched over his laptop, had me pausing at the doorway. I wasn't ready to deal with him yet. At least not until I had caffeine.

I heard banging in the basement, which at least gave me a neutral topic to start the day.

"What's that?"

The dark circles under Jake's eyes seemed almost drawn on, like the eye black that football players wear during games. "Zeke Harrison is downstairs. He offered to repair the sheetrock around the furnace room. I gave him a list of items in the shop to box up and deliver to Clark's auction gallery. Some they're buying outright, the rest will be on consignment. I'm organizing the backup documentation for the pieces."

I frowned. "Why?"

"It's customary to provide an auction house with authenticity documentation."

"No," I said, struggling to control my irritation. "Why are you having a fire sale?"

He shrugged. "Cash flow. The Heart boys may be unorthodox, but they're not cheap. I had to give Michael a $1,000 retainer to represent me and Harry is charging $250 per day for security."

I poured myself a cup of coffee, wondering if it was too early to add a shot of whiskey. "What are you keeping in stock? We can't have an empty shop when customers–"

Jake gave a short laugh. "What customers? Keeping the shop open is the least of my worries. Selling this stuff to Clark's gives us some room financially. I want to make sure that you–"

I interrupted him before he could finish. "So your plan is to close the business without even asking me?"

I was angry again. It was exhausting. "I guess that's your mode of operation. Your decisions, my life."

I got up and stalked out of the kitchen. I didn't want to go back to the bedroom, so I headed downstairs. At the very least, I would decide what antiques I wanted to keep. Maybe I'd open my own shop.

It was all so damn complicated.

The shop was empty when I walked into the main room. I noticed that the sheetrock still needed to be repaired. China sets, decorative urns, clocks, lined the counter. Almost every flat surface was covered with the antiques that Jake and I had so carefully selected. There were empty boxes and wrapping materials strewn on the floor. I checked in the furnace room, but it too was empty. Zeke didn't seem to have accomplished anything.

I noticed a light coming from the storeroom. I wandered over and peeked in. It was empty too, although several file drawers were open. I turned to go back into the shop and bumped into Zeke.

The trucker gave me a broad smile. "Morning Mrs. Cohen. Glad to see you home. How are you feeling?"

"Much better, thanks. I didn't see you when I came downstairs."

Zeke nodded. "No, ma'am. I was out checking my truck for more packing tape. I'm clean out. Going to have to get some more if Jake wants me to pack all this up."

"Why don't you finish the repair work on the sheetrock? I want to go over the list of antiques Jake plans to sell."

"Jake said–" Zeke protested.

"I know what Jake said. But I need a couple of hours to figure out what's to go and get the supporting documentation organized."

The trucker shrugged. "Okay, you clear it with Jake." He headed towards the furnace room.

***

I spent the next half-hour sorting through the antiques that Jake had selected to sell, getting angrier by the minute.

He was effectively closing the business. I hit the roof when I spotted the china set that belonged to his mother. It was Royal Crown Derby Asian Rose, one of the few things on which I agreed with the old battle-axe. It was delicate and gorgeous, and she had service for 24. Heck, a dinner plate alone was worth $175.

I stormed up the stairs. Jake was still in the kitchen, checking a site on the Internet and scratching notes on a yellow pad.

"You're selling your mother's china?" My voice probably carried to the next county. "While you're at it, where's the Waterford crystal?"

Jake held up his hands in defense. "You don't even like my mother."

"I like her china. She'll kill you for giving it to strangers."

Jake shrugged. "I'll handle my mother. The china alone will probably bring in $10,000. You'll be able to—"

I marched over to the table and slammed my hand down on the top. "Stop trying to pay me off."

Jake turned beet red. "I'm not. You'll need money to—"

"To do what? Start over? Probably, but I'm not doing it by selling your mother's wedding china. She'd never forgive me."

Jake ran a hand through his dark curls. "You're angry, hurt and scared. And most of that is my fault."

I laughed. "Maybe, but I know you're in the same boat, so to speak. Right now I can't even have a rational conversation with you, and I don't know if I even want to, because you're too busy selling the business so you can pay me off or bribe me or beg me to stay or punish yourself or–"

This time Jake laughed. "Or all of the above."

I sank down in a chair opposite him. I was exhausted. Any energy I'd had in the morning was long gone. I also hadn't taken my meds or eaten breakfast for that matter.

"I'm making some eggs and toast. Have you eaten?"

Jake put a hand on mine. "Let me do it."

I started to protest.

"Yes, it's guilt talking, but it's also me Jake taking care of Val, who's been hurt and is still sick."

I didn't have the energy to fight him. And yes, breakfast was the least he owed me.

While Jake moved from counter to refrigerator to stovetop, I studied the notes he'd made on the yellow pad. There were five columns marked: Item, Date Bought, Dealer, Price Paid, Sell For. I was surprised to find listed most, if not all, of Jake's World's Fair memorabilia. He'd been collecting it for years, long before we'd met. He once explained that he got interested when he inherited several pieces from his Great-Grandfather Bart who'd gone to the 1904 Louisiana Purchase Exposition, the Fair made famous by the movie *Meet Me in St. Louis.*

He slid a plate with a large vegetable omelet and rye toast in front of me. I got two forks and handed him one. He refilled my coffee cup and his. It was a familiar dance. It could almost have been a quiet Sunday. The kind we'd enjoyed before this nightmare began.

But I looked at the legal pad and knew it wasn't. "This is worse than selling your mother's china."

"Eat," he urged and took a half slice of the rye.

The omelet was good and I ate more than my half and a piece of toast. It was only when I pushed the plate away that Jake picked at the remains.

I wasn't sure where to begin. "You don't have to do this. When the police find the killer, you can go back to running your business. But not if you sell everything at bargain prices."

Jake blew out a breath. His voice sounded shaky. "Does that mean…mean that you know I'm not the killer?"

I shrugged. "Yes. I'm not sure how we're going to get past your betrayal, hell, it would have been easier to accept if you'd confessed to robbing banks or selling drugs before we met. Instead you sold me out for 30 pieces of silver and paraded your ex-lover in front of me for years without telling me about the relationship. But a killer? No, I know you couldn't kill someone."

Jake whispered. "I'm so very sorry, Val. As my Mother would say, it's all too little and too late. But if you'll let me, I'll spend the rest of my life trying to earn your trust again."

"Well, selling your mother's wedding china and your World's Fair collection isn't the answer."

Jake sighed. "I'll make you a deal. Let me sell the Fairchild dining room set. It's a quality 18th century set, fully restored, that will give us some wiggle room. I know

Clark's already has clients interested. It'll be fast and easy. The rest, we can talk about later."

I loved that old dining room set, but his reasoning made sense. "Okay."

I glanced down at the list of his World's Fair Memorabilia. He hadn't completed the information for most of the items. The name Corky appeared several times under Dealer. "Who's Corky?"

Jake laughed and this time it was one of delight. "He was my Great Uncle. Real name was Charles and I've got no idea why they called him Corky. I inherited a few pieces from him. Crazy as a loon, but a real sweetheart."

"Why does it matter who you bought an item from?"

"Another means of verifying its authenticity. Won't eliminate all fake reproductions, but it helps if I've dealt with a reputable dealer who knows his stuff. I've got to get better organized. A lot of the paperwork is still in the file cabinets downstairs. I want to transfer everything to a digital record."

"Jake?"

We hadn't realized that Zeke had joined us.

"I finished the sheetrock. It's taped, sanded, and ready for painting. What do you want to do about moving the antiques?"

The trucker glanced between us.

Jake stood up. "I've changed my mind about what we're selling, at least for now. Let's go downstairs. I'll show you the pieces to take to Clark's."

I started to pour myself another cup of coffee, but stopped. Too much caffeine would just make me jittery. There was something rolling around in my mind, just out of reach. Something Jake had said, but everything was a jumble. I needed a nap. I was tired of being tired.

*****

My head hit the pillow and I was out. No dreams, no nightmares, just deep, healing sleep. Or at least it would have been except I heard someone whispering my name.

"Val, Val, wake up."

I could barely open my eyes. Jake swam into focus. I turned over and put a pillow over my head. Hadn't the man said he needed to take care of me because I was sick and hurt?

"Go away."

"Val, listen to me. I think I'm on to something, but I need to talk to someone who won't think I'm crazy."

"You are crazy," I mumbled.

"Seriously, Val, I know you need your sleep, but just hear me out and tell me if this is a plot straight from one of those *National Treasure* movies you love–something that doesn't happen in real life."

I lifted the pillow off my head and squinted at the clock. I'd been asleep an hour. It didn't seem nearly enough. Slowly, I sat up and faced what looked like an over-excited puppy dog.

He began before I could even open both eyes. "Once I got Zeke underway, I sat down and made a list of what we know."

He waved his yellow pad in front of me.

I nodded slowly. First because I was still waking up and second, because I was trying not to resent the fact that he didn't recognize that when I was asleep it was a welcome respite from the horror movie we were living.

I shrugged. "Okay Sherlock, what do we know?"

He started to pace because Jake thinks better when he moves. "Let's go on the assumption that the killer has a purpose rather than this being just a killing spree."

"I don't understand."

"I think the killer wants something, some object or objects, and he kills when he either gets the object or when he gets the information he needs."

"What? How did you come to that conclusion?"

"Because he seems to be murdering certain types of people."

Maybe I was still trying to clear the cobwebs from my brains, but I couldn't follow his train of thought. "I still don't understand. What does the killer want and who are these people he targets?"

He ticked the victims off on his fingers. "What do the Changs, Newton, Margo, and Rudy have in common?"

I thought for a moment. "You?"

"Well, yes. There's that. But I think they also have antiques in common," Jake said.

"And dogs," I added. "Although did you check on the Bermans, did they have a dog?"

"Yes, a much beloved Irish setter. But I don't think that's the real connection. I mean the vet was the place where Rudy met his potential robbery victims, but I don't think Rudy got to the Bermans." He crossed his arms. "I think it's the antiques. That's the real connection."

I nodded, but thought of a problem. "What about the Bermans? You didn't know them and you didn't sell anything to them. I didn't see anything in the house to indicate they traded in antiques or had any special interest in them."

He frowned, then brightened. "I think–" He looked like he was figuring out a difficult math problem in his head. "I think that in the Berman case the connection is the antiques left over from the Changs. The Bermans bought the contents along with the house."

"Maybe." I nodded. "Go on. I'm listening."

He started to pace again, but I held up my hand. "Wait, sit down and talk to me. I'm getting dizzy watching you."

Reluctantly he sat on the bed. "Now if we agree that the common denominator is me and antiques, the next question is what specifically is the killer looking for."

I waved my hand. "Wait, Alicia told us. A map of Pennsylvania."

Jake grinned. "Right. But not just a map of the state, but a part of one, which leads me to believe that the killer has the other part or parts."

"Why would he kill for a map of Pennsylvania?"

He took a deep breath. "Okay, here's the leap of faith that I'm making. It's not a map of Pennsylvania, per se, it's a map of some specific place in the state."

"Like a city? Philadelphia? Is that where you got the idea? From the *National Treasure* movie that was set in Philly? The killer wants the Declaration of Independence?"

Jake shook his head. "No, I admit it's what made me think of it, but no, it's not a map of Philly or a city. I think it's a treasure map."

I rolled my eyes. "Come on. Get real. What kind of treasure? Gold doubloons? What pirate ship landed in Pennsylvania?"

"You're close. Civil War gold, lost in the forests of Cameron and Elk counties. I found a report on-line about how a Union army lieutenant was transporting a wagon that had been fitted with a false base. In the hidden compartment were 26 gold bars each weighing 50 pounds. When the soldier got sick and delirious with fever, he revealed the secret of the gold. The wagon and guards never made it to their destination and the gold was never found despite exhaustive hunts for it."

I was quiet for a few moments. It was a lot to digest. "That is one heck of a leap. The killer is looking for the gold?"

Jake agreed. "I know. But think about it. It has to be something really big for the killer to do everything he's done. Maybe it's a start?"

He wanted me to be excited about his great discovery. But in thinking about it, I wasn't sure that we'd learned much. He had merely said aloud what I hadn't quite put together. Somebody was willing to kill for something big. The rest was just guesswork. Maybe the theory about the gold was true; maybe not. But one thing was for sure. We had to find the missing piece of the map before the killer did. Our lives depended on it.

CHAPTER 27

"I wish we could go back and start over," Jake remarked as he waited for Michael Heart's secretary to track down her boss. "I wish we had met another way at another time, without all the baggage I brought to the relationship."

I glanced up from the boxful of receipts I was sorting. Jake's accounting during the shop's early years left much to be desired. I was looking at purchases he made during his first buying trip to Pennsylvania.

"Jake, that's a nice sentiment but doesn't really solve anything here and now." I looked back down at the unfiled paperwork. "Why haven't you logged these old purchases into a digital file? Sifting through this mess could take days."

"I always thought I'd catch up. But with Mother's illness and generating some cash flow to pay bills, I never got to it. Later, I hired an accountant to set up a tracking system that I could maintain. We just started with January of that year and I never looked back."

"Well we are looking back now. If we believe that a treasure map exists and that you purchased and/or sold the antiques that contain the map pieces, we have to figure out what they are. Alisha Warren said the killer wanted a silverware chest that they stole from Margo. I'm trying to see if you ever purchased one prior to the Changs murder."

"Val, I've probably purchased and sold a few dozen of them. They are in high demand and I'm always able to move them quickly. You know that."

He was right. We needed another way. "What if–"

Jake began speaking into his cell phone. Apparently Michael was finally on the line.

"What? Why?" Jake glanced at me. His expression was wary. "I don't know if Val will go for that or not. Yeah, I understand. Fully trained. But I've already paid you for...Okay. That's fair. Fine. I'll see you later."

Obviously, our attorney had more bad news for us. I waited for Jake to relay it.

He got up and started pacing, an almost impossible feat with all the boxes and stacked furniture taking up all the floor space.

"Jake!" I hadn't intended my tone to be that sharp but I was running low on patience. "What the hell is it now?"

"Harry had to go to Florida."

"What?" Harry Heart wasn't my favorite person in the world but I'd felt a lot safer with him standing guard at our house.

"Michael said his brother had an emergency and flew out of La Guardia an hour ago. Something about a "skip" and one of his bounty hunters in trouble. But the good news is that we're getting a full refund for the personal protection part of our contract."

I gripped the edge of the desk in preparation for what he was about to say next. "What's the bad news and I know there is bad news!"

"Michael has arranged for some private security for the house."

"And?"

Jake walked towards the stairs, calling back over his shoulder, "It's a guard dog."

"No. Jake, you call him back and tell him no. Jake, I mean it."

***

I was in a staring contest with a dog.

I stared at the German Shepard and he stared back at me. One of us was going to blink first and it wasn't going to be me.

"Come on, Val. It's not a pet. It's a trained guard dog. He'll go back when this is all over."

Michael cleared his throat. "Uh, about that."

"What?" Jake and I both turned and snapped the question at the attorney.

"In the rush of getting Harry to the airport...I misunderstood what Harry...Well, Harry didn't say what I thought he said. This particular dog is...well he's housebroken and knows the basic commands but he hasn't actually been qualified as a guard dog. He's more of a candidate for training."

I felt my face flushing with anger. "Of all the...are we paying for this dog's services?"

Michael shrugged. "No. Sorry. Actually I'll be paying you. Or Harry will. To dog sit. Harry got Houdini from a shelter and is in the process of training him. Since Harry is gone and you need someone...Actually this is all Harry's idea and you can call him on his cell phone."

"Michael, what in the world—"

"Sorry Val. I have to run. I've got a meeting with a judge on another case."

"Why is he called Houdini?" Jake asked, a smile on his face. I knew that look. In fact I wouldn't have put it past him to have set this whole scene up with Harry.

Michael pointed towards the spot near the sofa where the dog had been sitting a few seconds before.

Both Jake and I did a double take. The dog had disappeared.

***

"Do not get attached," I warned Jake, who was feeding the dog one of the pizzas that Harry had purchased for my homecoming from the hospital. "Houdini is just visiting."

My husband was obviously thrilled with our new security. Me, less so. In less than two hours the dog had managed to get his head stuck in a large urn, trapped himself under a metal coffee table, and gotten tangled up in the drapes in the living room. Just wait until Ruth Cohen got a look at those. I had no doubt that Jake's mother would provide better protection from intruders than that overgrown puppy. I made a mental note to pick up some pepper spray the next time I left the house.

We were back in the shop, sorting through the box of receipts. While we'd been searching for Houdini, Jake's earlier statement about starting over from the beginning played over and over in my mind. I wanted to apply that idea to the search for the antiques.

"Let's group the items by the original owner's names. I see some of your earliest Pennsylvania purchases were from the Calvin Weatherly estate. What do you remember about that sales trip?"

Jake held his hands out to the dog, letting him verify that there was no more pizza to be had. "It lasted ten days. I didn't take enough cash. My new hiking boots rubbed blisters on my heels."

"What else? What did you buy?"

"It was kind of embarrassing. First few days I purchased too much. Zeke got there with his moving van and I half-filled it before the big Weatherly estate sale even started. I think I ended up getting a U-Haul and bringing some of the Weatherly stuff, like that Civil War era trunk in the storeroom, back myself. Almost got a hernia loading the trunk. First time I'd ever pulled a trailer. Backing it up was a nightmare."

"Talk to me about the items you purchased, Jake. I don't care about your blisters or trailer backing skills."

"Hey, talking about that stuff is bringing back memories. And for your information, my backing up skills have evolved over the last ten years."

I hid a smile. "Evolved maybe, but improved? Remember when you offered to move Zeke's truck for him last month? I thought the man was going to have a heart attack."

"That's so unfair! He said it was an insurance thing."

Houdini gave a short bark. Jake took it as agreement with his side of the argument; I took it as a signal the dog need to go outside for a walk around a bush or two.

"Take Houdini outside and practice patrolling the perimeter. You can think about the trip while you're out there. Meanwhile I'm going to put all the Weatherly estate item receipts in one box."

***

An hour later I'd figured out the Changs ended up with the majority of the Weatherly estate items that Jake had purchased. Apparently his comment about "too much" applied to the stuff he'd bought from other dealers or the vendor booths in the antique malls. The Weatherly estate, the part Jake purchased, totaled little more than a dozen items, mostly large, expensive furniture pieces. The only way I discovered that was by the receipts, only half of which, such as the Chinese screen, were ever logged into Jake's inventory data base. Instead he had scribbled on the original receipts notes about the shop's resale of the item, when or if it happened. Some of the Weatherly antiques were still in the shop, years later, taking up space and collecting dust. I checked each one for clues about a map or the gold or even just anything odd, but came up with zilch, except for dirty hands.

Then I remembered the one other piece from the Weatherly estate. I went up to our bedroom. Jake had a few pieces of his World's Fair Memorabilia displayed on his dresser. I picked up the small St. Louis World's Fair jewelry box he'd kept from that buying trip. I took off the top, felt the inside for a hidden compartment, turned it over and over–and nothing. No magic drawer popped open. It was just an empty souvenir of a happier time.

I went back down to the basement and scoured the receipts again. One discovery of particular interest–Jake had purchased a silverware chest from the Weatherly estate. Inexperienced, he'd sold it a few months afterward for much less than it was really worth. A few months ago he had bid on a collection of World's Fair memorabilia. Included in the auction was the same silverware chest he'd acquired from the Weatherly estate. He'd lost the latest auction to Margo. Apparently the silverware chest was then stolen from Margo by the Warrens, who sold it to Newton548. Considering that Newton548, Margo, and Rudy Warren were now all dead, Jake's loss was a real blessing.

***

Jake knocked on our bedroom door before opening it a crack.

"Val? Are you awake? Houdini and I wanted to say goodnight."

I was sitting up in bed with my laptop, searching for information about Calvin Weatherly. There wasn't much. A native Pennsylvanian, Calvin had been an amateur historian and a Civil War buff. During his working years, he'd dabbled in stocks with money inherited from his great-grandfather Isa Benton. Isa Benton, a former Civil War soldier, had made his money in mining, and later manufacturing. Calvin had died without heirs, his wife Lien, having died 40 years prior in childbirth.

"I'm asleep," I said, scrolling down the Wikipedia page. I looked up when the dog jumped up on the bed and turned around in a circle twice before settling on the comforter.

Jake did the same, without the jumping and turning.

"Not happening," I mumbled, going back to reading the computer screen.

He scooted over so he could read along with me. "You think Weatherly is the key?"

"Yes. Is "Lien" a Chinese name?" I highlighted it so he could see the context.

He nodded. "Explains the Asian pieces."

"What was the name of the Union soldier who transported the gold? The one you were talking about the other day?"

"I don't think the article said."

I looked from the screen to him. "We should find out if it was Benton."

CHAPTER 28

"Lock the door and put on the alarm. Are you sure you won't let me leave Houdini with you?"

"Absolutely not." Houdini had a weak bladder and a short attention span. I had no intention of taking him outside every half hour all day long.

"You could come with me, just sit on Stan's sofa and nap or something."

"No. I'll be fine here. Maybe the killer has already found the missing map piece and is off digging for gold."

"What about Richard? He's still off-leash."

Houdini's ear pricked up at the mention of the word *leash*.

I struggled for patience. "Harry thinks Richard has left the state. He used a credit card in Reno a couple of days ago."

"Still, I wish you'd come with me."

"No. Frankly, Jake I'd appreciate some *alone* time to think through everything."

I knew Jake was loathe to leave me, but he needed to finish the job of appraising the antiques at Newton548's house. With the shop still closed, and no clear date to be re-opened, Jake hoped that Frank Freedman would give him the job of selling the valuable pieces in the estate in exchange for a commission. He'd agreed to meet Frank, after Frank got off work, at Newton's house.

"Okay." Jake sighed. "I probably won't be home until close to midnight. Get some rest. You're still recovering. Keep your cell phone handy. Call me if you need anything or you get a feeling that something isn't right." He'd adopted a fussing, mother hen voice, which I had grown to detest over the last few days.

A thought occurred to me. "You sure you want to go back to that house? Stan Freedman's ghost might–"

Jake waved me off. "Nah, don't worry about me. Houdini will protect me." He grinned.

"Don't start," I warned. "The dog is not staying."

"I know." Jake nodded, but I wasn't sure he was really in agreement with me over Houdini. I suspected Jake was just biding his time, waiting for me to weaken on the subject.

***

I dutifully locked up the house, switched on the alarm, and settled down with a glass of red wine and a bowl of popcorn, to watch *Rear Window*, the old Jimmy Stewart-Grace Kelly thriller that is scary, but worth it for the fashion alone. I deliberately sat in the wingback chair that was Jake's mother's favorite, knowing she could no longer bother me. It felt liberating when a little wine spilled on the seat cushion. I'd always hated the fabric.

I paused the DVD just when the nurse says, "He killed her in there, now he has to clean up those stains before he leaves."

Maybe watching a movie about a man who kills his wife wasn't such a good idea. I needed more wine. The light of the microwave digital clock served as a beacon for the bottle of chardonnay I'd left on the counter.

"I told you that I didn't like strangers in my house."

I jumped at least two feet in the air. It had been a few weeks since I'd last seen my mother-in-law. She looked as disgruntled as ever, hands on her hips, lips pursed.

"There are no strangers here, unless you're still calling me that. And FYI, it's not your house anymore."

Nothing like a near-death experience to empower you to take on the dead.

"Listen missy. It's because of you my son is in danger. You and your psychic powers got him mixed up with a killer who won't stop until my boy is dead."

"Hey, I'm not taking the blame for this." I took a sip of the wine. "Besides Jake is the one who lied to me when we first met. I don't even know him anymore. Maybe I never did."

"Regardless, he must have had his reasons. Now he's in danger. He could lose everything." She sniffed. "The killer is after you too, for that matter."

Ruth Cohen wasn't telling me anything I didn't know. "I've got the door locked and the alarm is on. Jake will be back in a couple of hours and then we're leaving town for a vacation. You can have the house to yourself."

"You'll never make it. That man will kill you first." She pointed to the dark hallway behind me.

A disembodied voice echoed around the room. "You really are as crazy as the newspapers said. You're talking to an empty room, Val. Nobody here but you and me, and just so you know, the alarm is off. "

My heart stopped. I whirled around looked in the direction Ruth had pointed. A large dark shadow loomed just beyond the light. I couldn't see his face, but I recognized the voice.

"Zeke, what are you doing here?"

I tried to keep my voice conversational, but couldn't disguise the tremor.

"Oh, Miz Cohen. You know exactly why I'm here. You can make this easy or...."

He stepped into the room, holding a knife, the last of the Chinese blades. I'd never gotten around to dumping it in the Sound. He must have taken it from my purse when he kidnapped me. "Or Val, you can make it hard. Either way, I get the map. Poor Jake will get the blame for your murder when the police find this knife."

My mind was still trying to fathom how he got in, ignoring what he planned to do. "I set the alarm myself."

Zeke rolled his eyes. "In front of me at least a dozen times. You really think it's that hard to remember the code ValZ?"

"But the door was locked." At that moment it was important to me to know exactly how he got in so I could stop him from doing it again. I was neatly forgetting that he didn't need to return once he got what he wanted.

Again, he rolled his eyes. His patience for my stupidity was limited. "You leave a key to the door hanging inside the closet. I borrowed it, made a copy, and saved it for the right occasion."

He smiled at his cleverness.

I glanced at the back door.

Zeke gave a small laugh. "Everyone thinks they can get away. Some tried to run. Some tried to beg. But you know how it turned out. So don't even try."

The phone rang shattering the silence. Caller-ID announced it was Jake on the phone.

"He'll be worried if I don't answer. He'll call the police. They would end up being his alibi."

Zeke shrugged. "Okay. Pick it up. Make it short. Like I said, you know the ending, but how painful it is, that's up to you."

I could barely hold the receiver in my shaking hand. "Hello."

Would he hear terror in my greeting?

Apparently not. "I'm finished. Not as much worth selling as I'd hoped. Want me to pick up a pizza on the way home?"

My stomach roiled at the thought. "No. Not hungry."

Zeke motioned with the knife for me to end the conversation.

"I'll see you...." My voice caught. Zeke put the point of the knife against my back. I took a deep breath.

"Gotta go. Your Mom's giving me the devil for spilling wine on her chair. Got to clean it up."

I hung up.

Zeke snorted. "What the Hell was that? Jake's mother is dead. I went to the funeral."

I shrugged, trying to act casual. I'd never win an Academy Award for the performance, unless it was for the role of terrified wife. "I always tease Jake about his attachment to his mother's stuff. Can't change a thing in this house. It's like she still lives here."

I wasn't prepared for Zeke to agree. "Yeah. I've seen him in action. Time I nicked a piece of that precious dining room table, man almost cried."

Jake sounded like a total wuss, but he was still my best hope.

Zeke shook his head, returning to the task at hand. Getting the map and killing me. "Where is the map?"

"The World's Fair jewelry box is upstairs, in our bedroom. That's what you want, isn't it? It came from the Weatherly estate." I wasn't sure what Zeke wanted. Or if he even knew at this point. But I figured that directing his attention to the jewelry box was a better distraction than arguing that I had no clue what he was talking about.

Zeke pointed the knife in that direction. "Let's go."

I moved slowly, hoping against all reasonable hope that Jake would miraculously appear. He'd have to have been teleported to get from Mt. Vernon to Seamont in anything less than 15 minutes, unless he was already calling me from the road.

Zeke shoved me and I stumbled. "I can't move too fast. Still recovering from our last go-round. That was you, wasn't it?"

"If your stupid husband had just forked over the map, might have saved me a lot of grief."

If I was supposed to feel sorry for his inconvenience, I didn't. I was starting to get angry, which was better than despair or fear.

"What did you do with my wedding band?"

He laughed. "What? You want to be buried with it?"

I turned to face him. "Yes, damn it, I do. Give it to me."

Zeke reached into his pocket and slapped the ring in my palm. "Diamonds are too small to be worth anything. Kind of cheaped out on you that husband of yours."

I slid the ring on my finger and for a fleeting moment, remembered the way Jake looked at me when he slipped it on my finger at our wedding. Another shove from Zeke and the memories disappeared in an instant.

We climbed the eleven steps to the second floor landing. I held on to the banister, not sure my shaky legs could support me. If I was going to die, I wanted some answers.

"How did you know about the map and the fortune?"

"Drivers are invisible to people like you." Disdain dripped from his voice. "You think I don't hear what you're talking about? That I can't look stuff up on a computer? I was just a dumb trucker to you and your husband and that bitch Margo."

"I never thought you were dumb." It bothered me that he would think I was prejudiced. As for me, I thought I was too stupid to live. I'd had no clue that Zeke, nice, polite Zeke, was a crazy killer. My insight into the great beyond had been of zero help.

"Doesn't matter. Look who's the smart one now."

We'd reached the landing. The staircase doubled back and there were four more steps to the second floor.

"So you figured it out when you were in New Hope with Jake all those years ago?"

Zeke grinned, like a kid who'd hit a homerun. "Yep. I read an old ledger that was in Calvin Weatherly's library. It was about the missing gold. It was written by the soldier who drove the wagon. The guy faked his illness. Buried the gold. The ledger mentioned the map. Old man Weatherly was a descendent of the soldier. There was a note scribbled on the last page. Weatherly wrote that he tore the map into four pieces for safekeeping. Hid the pieces in four of his favorite antiques. Marked the antiques with his initials. I thought it was just an old story, no truth to it. But then I found the first piece. It was just luck. The map piece fell out of a breakfront when I packed it up to ship here. I checked. His initials were etched on the bottom of the breakfront. The rest of the map pieces took some time to locate. I was lucky that Jake picked the right pieces to buy at that sale. The bad news was that I couldn't get to the rest of them. I waited for Jake to resell them, thought I'd grab them then, when I did the deliveries. Instead Jake either delivered them himself or had them shipped via FedEx. I caught a break when he mentioned selling one of the items I was looking for to the Changs. A large porcelain dragon figurine with jade eyes. I had to break it to get the second piece of the map out of it."

I shuddered remembering the murder scene. "Did you also get the third piece from the Changs?"

He shrugged, then continued. Proud of his work. "No. I thought it was there, but I couldn't find it that night. I had to stay away from the house during the murder trial. Later I tried again and almost got caught. I searched for years, trying to find all the items from the Weatherly estate. Tracking down the ones Jake didn't buy. Eliminating possibilities. Then I made a deal with Margo. Together we managed to find the third piece of the map in a silverware chest. Jake had sold the item on-line years ago without logging it into his inventory database. Margo found it on eBay. She claimed some Vet Tech stole it from her and resold it. I fixed that bitch, but good. Shame that you can't trust anyone anymore."

I was still thinking about what he'd said about Jake's inventory. "You were able to look through Jake's books?"

"Any time I wanted. Jake should change his passwords and refrain from writing down the new one on his desk calendar." Zeke smiled. "That great accountant that set up Jake's system? Another cousin of mine. Problem was Jake didn't let my cousin enter all the old stuff. Cheap SOB. The old stuff was what I was interested in. Mattie even tried to do it for free, but Jake refused."

"Another cousin?" I wondered how many of those Zeke had. How many we had hired to do Zeke's bidding. Stupid, but I had the sudden worry that maybe his plumber cousin didn't know what the hell he was doing. We couldn't afford to pay someone else now. "Our plumber? Is he really a plumber?"

Zeke just laughed.

We'd reached the second floor. Our bedroom was at the end of the hall.

I flipped on the hall light, but one bulb was out in the overhead. I'd been pestering Jake for weeks to fix it. Not that it mattered anymore.

"How did you know that Jake had the fourth antique? The last piece of the puzzle?"

"The pair of you aren't too smart, you know. I just checked his notes downstairs. I saw that he'd figured out that I wanted the Weatherly stuff and that he'd kept the 1904 World's Fair jewelry box for himself. The old Weatherly ledger said the last map piece was safely hidden under the World's Fair Emblem."

I spoke without thinking. "But I've examined the jewelry box. There's nothing there. The only map is on the emblem itself; a small image of the Louisiana Purchase area."

Zeke stopped and grabbed my arm. "What do you mean there's nothing there? That was the only piece of World's Fair memorabilia that Weatherly had. You trying to hold out on me, stupid woman? Do you want to end up like Margo?"

He backhanded me and I fell against the wall. That was the third time he'd done that to me. Or was it the fourth? I was damn tired of it either way. I swallowed my anger for the moment.

"No, no. Zeke, you can have the jewelry box. Maybe you can find the map."

Just then, we heard the front door open. "Val, you there? What the hell? The door's open. The alarm's off. Are you crazy?"

Jake had made record time coming home.

Zeke turned towards the stairs, taking his eyes off me for a second.

"Jake," I screamed. "Run! Call the cops. The killer's here. It's Zeke."

Zeke turned to grab me, but I was already running down the hallway. I dashed into my bedroom and slammed the door. I fumbled with the old lock and finally it clicked, but it wouldn't hold long against a guy as big and angry as Zeke.

I grabbed the jewelry box and tucked it in my sweater pocket. Zeke was pounding on the door. Hiding wasn't an option. There was only one way out. I raced to the window and flung it open. I paused a second to reconsider, if I miscalculated, I was dead. If I didn't jump, I was dead.

The banging on the door got louder.

I had no choice. Perhaps my dreams about the tree were to prepare me for this moment.

Just as I leaped from the sill towards the largest branch, I heard the door break down.

"You're going to be sorry. I would have made it easy on you. With me knowing you all these years, I was going to be quick about it, as a favor."

My fingers caught hold of the rough bark, slick with half-melted snow. I was hanging more than 30 feet off the ground. I kind of expected my life to flash in front of my eyes or for my last thoughts to be about all I hadn't done yet in life. Instead I got this crazy vision of me and Jake's mother haunting the Cohen house and each other for eternity. Some things were too horrendous to even consider. I knew then that dying wasn't an option.

My grip slipping, I found the strength to swing a leg up and over the branch and pull myself into a sitting position on top. I sat on the branch, holding to the smaller limb just above it and caught my breath. The next step was to get down, but how? A controlled descent was my preference. It had been more than twenty years since I'd climbed up a tree, much less down one. My mind was racing, trying to figure out whether to attempt to climb down on my own or wait for the cops and a ladder.

"Where's the box, Val? Where's the box?"

I could hear Zeke trashing my bedroom, muttering to himself. I prayed that Jake had left the house and that the cops were on their way.

Suddenly, Zeke was standing on the window sill, his hand outstretched, almost able to touch the tip of the limb. I scooted as far back on the branch as I could go, stopping only when my body was flush against the trunk.

"Give it to me." I could see from his expression that he'd come too far, done too much, to leave the jewelry box behind.

I understood then what I needed to do to end this ordeal.

I dug in my pocket with one hand and held out the box, deliberately keeping it just a little too far away for him to grab.

"Zeke, I'll toss it to the ground. Leave now before the police get here and you can get it."

He growled like a wounded animal. He waved his knife in the dark night air. "I'm going to slice you so nobody will recognize you. There will be tiny pieces of Val scattered all over this place."

I was trembling so hard I could barely keep myself on the branch. My fingers were numb, from cold, from fear, it didn't matter. I stared into his eyes and in slow motion, my hand opened. The World's Fair Jewelry box went tumbling to the ground.

Zeke tried to grab it in mid-air. He almost had it, but the momentum of reaching so far out the window, unbalanced him. He grabbed for the frame, for the wall, for the branch, for anything to hold onto, but came up with air. In a flash, I understood my dream. The little boy who flew from the window. It wasn't my baby; it was Zeke.

He fell, his arms splayed wide, the Chinese knife, still in his right hand. I saw his face as he tumbled. There was a look of surprise, not fear. Maybe he thought he could fly. Maybe he thought he'd land and come back to kill me.

But right before he hit the ground, he brought his arms close to his body. The knife went right through him when his body landed with a muffled thud in the snow. He never made another sound.

***

It was 4:30 in the morning. I was both exhausted and wide awake. The Medical Examiner's truck had just pulled away, crime scene tape fluttered in the wind, and the neighbors had retreated into their own homes. Michael Heart, who'd we called once the police had arrived, conferred with the cops, assured us that the case against Jake would be closed, and thankfully took a very scared Houdini home with him. The dog's career as a guard dog seemed unlikely. He'd cowered under a bush once he saw the flashing lights of the patrol car.

Diane Ellison sat on the wing chair nursing her third or fourth cup of coffee. I sat as close as humanly possible to Jake on the sofa.

"So many questions," I mumbled. I didn't have the energy to ask them, but I desperately wanted answers.

"Go ahead, ask." Diane took another sip of coffee, made a face, and put the mug on the coffee table.

"Here's one. Was Zeke Harrison on the police's radar?" That was a question I wanted an answer to. Even if I hadn't even remotely considered him, even if my super powers were less than spectacular, did the cops have any reason to suspect the guy who had brutally slaughtered seven people? Jake had seen Stan Freedman's ghost and we knew the truth, even if the police didn't recognize that particular murder in their body count total. I was so busy considering the possibilities, I almost missed Diane's answer.

"Believe it or not," she smiled ruefully, "We'd pretty much missed Zeke. Yeah, I know, we pretty much missed a lot. The only thing I can say in our defense is that he was very clever and was until recently working with Margo so she was a good cover for his activities."

"Until she decided to get even greedier." It was the first time Jake had said anything for several hours. He was so pale that I was tempted to call a doctor. He'd passed on coffee and been nursing and refilling a Scotch ever since I'd climbed down the tree, via a Fire Department ladder. "She managed to fool everyone, most of all, me."

Was he regretting a lost love or simply the fact that he'd been a fool? It was a question for another time.

Diane shrugged. "I will say that we had begun to piece together that this was a bigger operation, that there was more involved than just the artifacts that were stolen."

I looked at the pieces of the coveted World's Fair Jewelry Box on the table. It had shattered in the fall. The cops hadn't seized it as evidence.

"The irony," and I wondered if that was the right word for it, "the irony is that the missing piece of the map isn't there. It's still out there."

Jake put one arm around my shoulders and sang, "Fifteen men on the dead man's chest–Yo-ho-ho, and a bottle of rum!"

I took his glass of Scotch and put it on the coffee table.

Jake laughed, a little wildly. "Don't you see? There's no guarantee that there ever was lost Union gold. Folks love long-lost treasures stories. It's like hitting the jackpot in Vegas. Just one tug on the one-armed bandit and Poof! You're a millionaire. Except it almost never happens which is why the House always wins. This whole sorry, tragic mess could just be Calvin Weatherly playing a stupid trick on gullible people. I need to find out what Zeke did with that journal he mentioned to Val. There may be an explanation in it. I don't know why Zeke was so convinced that the jewelry box held the fourth piece if it ever existed."

Jake reached for his Scotch, then stopped himself.

Diane stood up and stretched. "Obviously we're going to be searching Zeke's house for evidence. I'll let you know what we find. In the meantime, the two of you need to get some sleep."

I sighed. "Can we go away for a few days? That was our plan before all Hell broke loose."

Diane nodded. "Just leave me your contact information."

I yawned. Maybe I would be able to sleep.

Jake walked Diane to the door. I heard him throw the lock.

He came back in and looked around. I wasn't sure what he was searching for.

"This house..." he began.

"Is our home." I said firmly. "I refuse to let psychos drive me out of this money pit which I love."

Jake laughed and this time, it was genuine. He opened his arms and I quickly moved into them.

"By the way, those psychos include your mother." I mumbled into his jacket.

Another laugh and it felt so good. I had some thoughts about the missing map and the Civil War era trunk in the storeroom. It had loads of travel stickers on it. I wondered if one was from a trip to the St. Louis World's Fair. But any further searches could wait.

He tightened his grip. "Come on. We'll sleep in my grandparents' room tonight, hit the road tomorrow, and figure everything else later."

We walked up the steps, heading for the third floor when I realized something. "I'm actually not so tired anymore."

He grinned. "Me either."

The End

AUTHOR NOTES

Evelyn David is the pseudonym for Marian Edelman Borden and Rhonda Dossett. Marian lives in New York and is the author of twelve nonfiction books on a wide variety of topics ranging from veterans benefits to playgroups for toddlers! For more information on her books, please visit her website at:

www.marianedelmanborden.com

Rhonda lives in Muskogee, Oklahoma, is the director of the coal program for the state, and in her spare time enjoys imagining and writing funny, scary mysteries. Marian and Rhonda write their mystery series via the Internet. While many fans who attend mystery conventions have now chatted with both halves of Evelyn David, Marian and Rhonda have yet to meet in person.

Please check out Evelyn David's website and blog at:
http://www.evelyndavid.com
http://www.thestilettogang.blogspot.com/

BOOKS BY EVELYN DAVID

Sullivan Investigations Mystery Series
Murder Off the Books
Murder Takes the Cake
Murder Doubles Back
Riley Come Home - short story
Moonlighting at the Mall – short story

Non-Series Mysteries
Zoned for Murder
Mind Over Murder

Brianna Sullivan Mysteries
I Try Not to Drive Past Cemeteries
The Dog Days of Summer in Lottawatah
The Holiday Spirit(s) of Lottawatah
Undying Love in Lottawatah
A Haunting in Lottawatah
Lottawatah Twister
Missing in Lottawatah
Good Grief in Lottawatah
Summer Lightning in Lottawatah
Lottawatah Fireworks
Leaving Lottawatah

Romance Stories
Love Lessons

www.ingramcontent.com/pod-product-compliance
Lightning Source LLC
Chambersburg PA
CBHW060350260626
47160CB00006B/2262